I0626717

**SAM CRESCENT & STACEY ESPINO**

**EVERNIGHT PUBLISHING ®**

**www.evernightpublishing.com**

# BROKEN BASTARD

## Copyright© 2017

### Sam Crescent & Stacey Espino

Editor: Karyn White

Cover Artist: Jay Aheer

ISBN: 978-1-77339-323-0

## ALL RIGHTS RESERVED

# SAM CRESCENT & STACEY ESPINO

# BROKEN BASTARD

## *Killer of Kings, 2*

### Sam Crescent & Stacey Espino

### Copyright © 2017

### Chapter One

"Scarlett, are you being serious? No, I know you're not being serious, because if you were, you'd be insane," said Lisa.

"I have no choice. You heard Carter. He's going to cut twenty freelancers this year alone." Scarlett hooked her oversized purse over her shoulder, and then reached for the stack of colored file folders. "I can't lose this job."

"Fine, I get it, but this is suicide."

Scarlett rolled her eyes. "You're being dramatic."

She made her way to the office elevator, her friend tailing behind her. Her next interview might be unorthodox, and theoretically a bit dangerous, but desperate times called for desperate measures. She'd only been at this company for eight months, officially still on probation, so she'd be one of the first her boss would cut. Scarlett was damn good at what she did. One day she hoped to reach reporter level, but right now she had to give the stories she always found to someone else. The truth was, her boss *took* the stories she'd researched and gave them to other girls. Still, she was determined to show her worth, and how valuable she could be as a reporter.

It wasn't easy getting a personal meeting with Alexei Semenov. He was a big-time crime ringleader, not the biggest, but it would still be headline news. Her boss, Wilson Carter, had to see her value after closing an interview with a name like Semenov. Scarlett was sick and tired of pinching pennies and fighting just to maintain the status quo. She wanted to make something of her career, not to mention she didn't have enough money for next month's rent.

"Are you taking a camera crew?" asked Lisa, holding the elevator door open with her hip.

"Yeah, like that's going to happen. Look, I'll be fine. Promise. Semenov wants to portray a favorable image to the media, so he's going to be on his best behavior."

Lisa sighed. "You're impossible. See you tomorrow then? I'll bring the coffee."

"Thanks."

The doors began to close, and Scarlett watched her friend disappear from view. She wouldn't admit that her heart raced like a freight train, and her hands felt clammy. If she wasn't in such a dire predicament, there was no way she'd be heading out to meet one of the most hated men in the city. The man was a Russian mobster, and she had no wingman, camera crew … nothing.

Forty minutes later, she stopped her Kia Rio in front of a set of massive iron gates. She double checked the address she'd scribbled on a piece of paper, but this was definitely the place. The gates began to open, swinging inwards, so she continued to drive along the long path. She admired the manicured grounds, water fountains, and old-world architecture of the mansion coming into view.

She took a deep breath as she parked the car. *You can do this, Scarlett.*

The sky started turning a mix of orange and pink, signaling the sunset was fast approaching. She didn't like meeting at night, but she couldn't get off work early and Mr. Semenov insisted they meet at eight o'clock sharp.

Scarlett lugged all her supplies out of the passenger side. She'd brought an older model video camera with tripod, voice recorders, paperwork, and her laptop. This was a huge deal, so she wore her best suit, reserved for only the most important occasions. The wine-colored skirt and jacket did a great job at concealing her explosive curves. Her extra weight was only another reason she had to make this work. Wilson Carter only kept the young, thin girls at the front of the house, and the same was true for the news and weather editions of his cable network.

As she walked up the custom stone staircase toward the entry doors of the house, she was flanked by Alexei Semenov's security detail. She held her breath as they approached her.

"I have an appointment at eight o'clock for an interview," she said before being asked. Scarlett swallowed hard after speaking. The three men didn't smile, their faces solemn as they glared at her with enough malice to make her question her decision to come. One of the men snatched her bags away from her and began rooting through them, while another patted her down like a common criminal.

"Mr. Semenov will see you in the sitting room." Then he opened the door and motioned for her to enter. The foyer was bigger than her entire apartment, with vaulting ceilings and shiny white marble floors. There was enough artwork and stone sculptures in view to fill a small museum. She walked forward, in complete awe. No reporter had been through these doors, so she was one of the privileged few to see the inside the Semenov mansion. It probably helped that she wasn't a reporter, and there was no mention of her in any of the articles she had been part of, not even as a researcher. She was a nobody, fighting to be a somebody.

"Sit here," said another man, pointing to one of the sofas. "He will be with you shortly."

She nodded and sat down, resting her bags by her feet. Within minutes she was alone in the sitting room. The place was quieter than a mausoleum. Scarlett tapped her foot, her nervous energy not letting up. The doors to a study were partially open ahead of her, the glow from a desk lamp catching her attention. Should she take some pics? She didn't want to do anything that might get her into trouble, so she didn't risk it. Instead, she began to attach the tripod to the clunky old video camera in preparation for the interview. After today, maybe they'd trust her with the newer equipment.

At just a few minutes to eight, a couple men in suits rushed down the hallway, brandishing handguns. She gasped and froze. There was commotion just out of sight, and then a gunshot shattered a large clay vase, the shards raining down on the marble. Scarlett dropped to her knees and crawled to the end of the sofa to hide. *Oh God, why didn't I listen to Lisa?*

The doors to the study flung open, and a huge man in a navy suit stood in the entryway with an automatic weapon in both hands. He looked like the damn Terminator. She heard different men yelling in Russian but couldn't understand a word. The big man didn't even take a step before he collapsed to the ground after another gunshot rang off, the sound echoing in the massive sitting room. Then she saw him, Alexei Semenov, coming around from the grand oak desk in the office. Scarlett recognized him immediately. His stern, wrinkled face was always plastered on the news.

*What the hell is happening?*

Alexei spoke in a cool but arrogant tone, in his own language. Who was he talking to? Then a different man dressed in all black strode toward the office. He came out of nowhere, like a ghost. She noticed the hand holding his gun was covered in ink. In fact, the tattoos even peeked out from the top of his collar, climbing up his neck. He looked like a force, death personified. The two men spoke briefly, a calm exchange, and then she watched as the tattooed man put a single bullet between Alexei's eyes. It all seemed to happen in slow motion— the gunshot, the spray of blood, the lifeless body crashing to the floor.

Scarlett let out a scream but quickly covered her mouth with both hands. It was too late. The killer turned his head and looked directly at her crouched down at the end of the sofa.

He cursed, holstering his weapon, and came toward her. She screamed again, toppling back onto her ass.

"Shut up," he said, yanking her to her feet.

"I'm innocent. Please don't hurt me..."

He noticed the video camera equipment on the sofa, and it set him off. With a powerful thrust, he smashed it against the stone floor and stomped it out of existence.

"You one of his whores?"

She struggled to speak, completely tongue-tied, so she shook her head. He growled, glancing around the ceiling of the room before grabbing a handful of her suit jacket and tugging her along with him. They ended up in a small, windowless room with wall to wall surveillance equipment. Probably every room in the house was being filmed on the small televisions, including every angle of the property. He took something out of his jacket, slapping it down on the desk. He hunched over, but she couldn't see past his massive frame. When he stood back up, she saw the explosive device with a timer rigged to it. Forty-five seconds and counting.

She stared with her mouth agape. Was she dreaming? No, this was definitely a nightmare, one she wished she could wake up from. Things like this didn't happen to women like her. Scarlett could imagine the headlines now: *Thirty-six-year-old spinster dies grisly death, leaving behind no one and nothing.* God, how pathetic. She nearly began to cry thinking of all the life she'd wasted. At least someone at her office would get a headline story out of this mess, but it sure wouldn't be her.

Before she could react, he pulled her through the hallway, shooting every man that came into view with the pistol in his free hand. When they were in the parking area, the bomb in the surveillance room went off, the ground quaking beneath her feet. She flailed, but he had an iron grip on her arm. When she saw her piece of shit car, she wondered if she could get free long enough to make a break for it. Then she remembered her keys were in her purse, still in the sitting room.

"Please let me—"

"Don't fucking speak," he warned, his voice deep and authoritative. He popped open the trunk of a black BMW and shoved her in. She screamed and kicked, but he only slammed the trunk down over her, blanketing her in darkness.

**** 

*Fuck! Fuck!*

This was Bain's first official contract working for Killer of Kings, and he'd wanted to prove himself a valuable asset. He knew the rules: no witnesses and a clean hit, nothing unusual from his other work. Bain wanted to send the woman in his trunk straight to hell, but she didn't look like she belonged at Semenov's place. Cops didn't give a shit about dead criminals, but an innocent victim would lead to investigations and news reports. If it got back to Boss that his mission wasn't clean, he'd look like a fucking amateur.

So his witness was going to disappear without a trace, and nothing would be linked back to him or to Semenov's assassination. He still wasn't sure what the fuck he was going to do with her, but he'd figure that out later. Killing was what he did best, and he'd handled worse complications. Bain drove a few miles up the road, then got out to remove the false magnetic plates. He opened the trunk to toss them inside, ignoring his human cargo. She gasped when she saw him, although with no street lights on this stretch of road, he'd be a dark shadow. Not that it mattered if she saw him clearly or not because he wasn't letting her live.

"I'll do anything. Please let me go. I promise I won't say anything."

She definitely wasn't one of Semenov's girls. Bain had been scoping out his interactions and routines the past week, and the old bastard preferred his bitches stick thin and highly processed. His witness had thick curves and not a stitch of makeup—definitely not Semenov's type. He wasn't sure what she was doing there—maybe applying to scrub the toilets or some other domestic shit. Then he remembered the camera equipment.

"Why were you at Alexei Semenov's house?"

"I was just on a job, I mean I was doing an interview ... well I was going to do an interview," she stammered. "I'm a reporter. Well, I'm a researcher trying to be a reporter. I swear I don't know him or you or anything about what happened."

Of all the damn luck. A reporter, researcher, whatever the hell that meant.

"Who knows you were there?"

"Nobody."

He didn't believe a word she said. For all he knew there would be a media frenzy tomorrow. He'd have to keep her breathing until things settled down. Once he was sure her disappearance wasn't an issue, he could finish her off and burn the remains at the dump a couple counties over.

"You should have stayed home." He locked her back in the trunk.

Bain had a house in the rural area outside the city. He didn't like noise, people, or distractions. He valued his privacy.

After his contract with Bernard Sutherland went bad, Boss had shown up at Bain's house uninvited. He wasn't sure how the fuck he got his address. Bain had refused to work for Killer of Kings when Viper signed on years ago, not comfortable being under anyone's control. But Boss wasn't ready to give up, offering him the kind of cash he couldn't refuse.

No one else popped by to pay a visit. Salesmen were greeted with a shotgun, and soon no one dared to set foot on his property. His house wasn't luxurious. It was a shitty, century farm house that had been deserted and sold off in a power of sale. He liked that it was off the grid, open concept, and surrounded by acreage. There was no way he could live in a cramped condo or row housing. The confinement of city living didn't suit him.

He unlocked the front door and disabled his security system. It cost more than the damn house. Bain dropped his duffel bag on the slab kitchen table and unzipped it. He'd only used his handguns today, so it wouldn't take him long to clean them. All his weapons were well maintained, clean, oiled, and precision tested. This contract had been easier than he expected. Easy money was always a good thing. Then he remembered the woman in his trunk, and his mood soured.

Bain pounded his fist on the table, the weapons clanging together in the bag. Just thinking of her pissed him off. He hated complications.

He shrugged off his jacket, and then grabbed a black garbage bag from the cupboard and returned to the car. There were few stars in the sky, the darkness only cut when the light in the trunk clicked on. He stared down at the woman. Sweat matted her hair to her cheek, and even the minimal lighting made her squint. She held her forearms in front of her face in a defensive posture.

Bain shoved the bag over her head and heaved her out of the trunk. "Walk. If you try anything stupid, I'll kill you."

She kept quiet as he led her into his house. This was the first female in his place. When he fucked around, he did it anywhere else. Those occasions were few and far between. He was raised in hell itself, forced to seduce and fuck rich, older women so his captors could bribe them or get closer to their husbands' money. Sex had become something he hated, a punishment. He preferred the brutal beatings over the nights in strange beds, knowing he often had to murder the women he'd been forced to deceive.

Once inside, he locked the door and led her to the basement. He never went down there, but he wasn't going to keep this bitch under foot, so it was going to be her home until he decided otherwise. Bain thought about how much he hated women, but that wasn't true—he hated everyone. The whole world was against him, and even God abandoned him long ago.

The wooden stairs leading into the basement were

rickety, each step punctuated with a groan or creek. There was only one lightbulb swinging from the ceiling, barely lighting up the damp space. Once they were on the concrete floor, he tugged the garbage bag off her head and tossed it aside. She gasped for air, brushing her hair off her face. Her eyes were wild with panic, a look he'd seen too many times to count.

"Where are we?" she whispered.

"It's your final destination. No hard feelings, but damn, you were in the wrong place at the wrong time."

She hugged herself. "What are you going to do to me?"

"Relax. I'm not raping you," he said, insulted. Bain could get any pussy he wanted. He didn't need to kidnap women just to get laid.

"Please let me leave."

"That's not happening." He pulled an old wooden chair from the darkness and set it against the wall. "Keep quiet down here. If you annoy me, you won't eat."

"But—"

"I don't think you understand how this works. It's very simple. You do as I say or things go bad for you. Behave yourself, and you'll get food and bathroom privileges."

He wanted to get the fuck upstairs, the dankness already creeping along his skin. There were a few facts he needed from the woman—her name, family history, basic description. It would help him keep tabs on the news reports and aid him in digging deeper if he needed to.

Bain took a section of hair that had escaped her loose bun and felt it between his fingers. Then he tilted her chin up and took a good look at her—brown hair and green eyes.

"What's your name?"

"Scarlett."

"Scarlett what?"

"Scarlett Meyers."

"You married? Kids?"

She shook her head.

"Your parents work for the government?"

Scarlett narrowed her eyes. "No, why does any of this matter? I'm nobody. I'm not a threat to you or anyone."

He put a finger to his lips. "Who do they work for?"

"I don't know."

Bain grabbed her jacket and gave her a quick jerk. "Hey, I asked you a fucking question."

Her eyes welled up with tears. "I don't know! My dad left when I was six, and I haven't talked to my mom in years."

*Good.* The fewer people looking for her, the better. He pressed her shoulder down to get her to sit on the chair, then squatted down and patted her hips, feeling for pockets. "You have any weapons on you?"

"No."

His cell phone rang, so he stood back up and walked away from her.

"You get the job done?" asked Boss.

"I always get the job done."

"That's what I like to hear. I have another contract for you. Interested?"

Killing was all he knew. From the planning stage, surveillance, to pulling the trigger, it was all a rush. Something dark resided in him, for as long as he could remember, and it seemed his job as a mercenary was the only thing that kept it sated.

"Sure, why not?"

"Excellent. Now that Viper's retired, I'm short a

good man. You can go far with Killer of Kings, Bain."

Bain wasn't worried about the next paycheck or maintaining a lavish lifestyle. His life was no frills. He also had so much fucking cash that he was already set for life. He did his job because he had to.

"*Help me!*"

He whirled around. The little bitch had some nerve. Bain glared at her, his jaw twitching with his rising anger.

"Who was that?" asked Boss.

"Don't worry about her. You're not the only one I work for," he said, dismissively. "Text me the details. I'll be busy for a while." He put his phone in his pocket and crossed his arms over his chest. There were so many wicked things he could do to Scarlett to make her pay for her disobedience. He'd doled out every kind of torture in his day, most learned from personal experience. Right now, all he cared about was ensuring she kept quiet while he was away on his next hit. With his luck, someone would come to his front door and hear her screaming.

"You've been a bad girl, Scarlett."

She stared at him, her big green eyes roaming over his body. He looked down at himself. Over the years he'd gotten so much fucking ink that there wasn't much skin left untouched. It was a necessity, his way of covering up the past, an attempt to change himself into something new. It was never enough, the scars and memories continuing to haunt him.

"What do you think I should do to you for that little stunt?"

Her mouth opened, then closed. "I didn't mean it."

"Of course you did. You're trying to save yourself, but what you don't realize is there's no escape. Nobody knows where you are, and by the sounds of it, nobody gives a shit."

"You're never letting me leave?"

"There you go, now you're catching on. But until I can trust you, I'm sure you understand why I have to use this." He pulled out a black gag from his back pocket, waving it in front of her, and then motioned her to walk up the stairs. There was no way he could stand coming down into the shitty basement to check on her every few hours. The dank space was worse than he remembered, so he'd keep her within arm's length for now.

When they got to the top of the stairs, she made a break for it.

## Chapter Two

Scarlett tried to run, but he caught her around the arm and hauled her back against him. She fought hard. Fighting him was useless, but she couldn't stop. She needed to get away from this monster, to survive. Her life was miserable, but she didn't want to die. There was so much she hadn't achieved yet, and so much to live for.

Even her dismal love life was worth fighting for, wasn't it?

"Will you fucking stop!"

"Leave me alone."

"I told you to stay fucking silent, and you wouldn't listen, so now you're going to be quiet."

By the time the gag was over her mouth, her back was pressed against him, and during their little fight, he had somehow grabbed her breast, using it as something to hold onto. She didn't know exactly what happened next as she just froze up.

He had paused behind her, and all she heard was the sound of their breathing.

"Right," he said. "That's better. All silent right now, which is exactly how I like you." He released her breast, and dumped her into a chair. Any chance of escaping was lost as he tied her to that, too, a rope firmly around her waist.

Once she was secured to the chair, he clapped his hands once, and she watched as he went to his fridge, and started to make himself some food.

"Killing makes me hungry. What about you?"

She stared at him, unable to answer.

"Just so you know, my name is Bain," he said, and she watched as he grabbed two slices of bread, slathering one slice with peanut butter and the other with some kind of cream cheese. What a disgusting combination.

Tears filled her eyes as he lifted up one gun, and did some weird back and forth game with it. He knew his guns, and soon he was going to kill her.

Slapping the two slices of bread together, he rounded the counter to stand in front of her. She didn't mean to but ended up staring down at his crotch. Why was she staring at this man's dick? This was completely insane, and she didn't need this right now. The story she was going to tell had already gone up in smoke. Her life was ruined, and no one was going to hire her. She had reached her limit.

Bain cupped her chin and tilted her head back. "Why are you crying?"

She shook her head. She wasn't about to fight the damn band across her mouth to tell this brute exactly what was wrong with her. Once he found out that she had lied, and someone knew exactly where she was, Lisa was going to die. *Damn it.* All she'd wanted to do was keep her job and to show she wasn't just some researcher, but an actual reporter. She had lost count of the number of times her ideas had been taken by other women.

Every time she saw her story on the news she knew it had been given to someone else just because she wasn't young enough, or pretty enough, or slim enough. The media was a fickle place, and you either fit into a certain image or you worked out of sight at a shitty desk. She had been struggling for a long time.

She knew what it took to make a living, and she knew how to do her damn job.

He grabbed the gag that was in her mouth and pulled it off. "I was speaking to you."

"Why should I answer your questions? You're nothing but a murderer."

She tensed up expecting him to hurt her, but he only tilted his head to the side, and then sat down, eating his sandwich.

"You're not someone I would picture as a reporter."

Scarlett said nothing, trying to deal with whatever insult he was cooking up.

"You're beautiful," he said and that had her looking at him. No one had ever called her beautiful before. At thirty-six years old, she was past being beautiful, and sometimes a boyfriend had told her she was pretty or that she was okay. Yeah, the total sum of her compliments was being told that she was okay. She could live with that though. Staring at this man, this killer, as he told her that she was beautiful seemed so absurd. "What were you doing at Alexei Semenov's house?"

"I told you already. I'm a researcher, I mean … reporter."

Bain stared at her, taking another bite of his sandwich as he watched her. "Why him?"

She licked her lips and glanced past his shoulder. The tears that she had been keeping at bay for so long finally came to and dropped down her cheeks. "They're making cutbacks at work. I'm not getting any younger, and we know that Alexei Semenov is a criminal. I wanted to interview him. No one would dare book an interview with him. Not only did I do that, but I actually got a sit down with him. I got the chance of a lifetime."

"You know he would have never allowed a bad word said about him."

"Why did you have to kill him?" she asked.

"Simple. He had a hit out on his head, and I'm known for taking care of that."

"Ugh, you should just kill me now. There's no

way I'm going to be able to get another job."

He chuckled. "You're funny."

"Great. Now I'm entertaining a psycho. This day couldn't get any worse."

"What's funny is you thinking you can get away. I've got news for you, princess. You're not leaving this place alive, so you can either give me a reason to keep you around and alive, or you're going to be dead very soon."

She was terrified. The calm way he gave her a death sentence—no one should be able to do that, and yet he seemed so calm, so deadly, and it was all wrong.

"You're really going to kill me?"

"Yeah, probably. It depends who else I'm going to have to kill. I've got a feeling you're a smart woman, Scarlett. Something tells me that you're not stupid enough to go to a known criminal's house without saying something to someone."

She kept her thoughts to herself, praying that Lisa just forgot about her. She had thought she was being clever, and only now she saw the error of what she had done. Now she was regretting everything.

Bain finished his sandwich and stood up. "Do you like peanut butter?"

"What?"

"Peanut butter? Do you like it? That's all you're getting."

"I thought I wasn't allowed to eat," she said.

He glared at her. "Do you want some fucking food or not?"

"Yes, I like peanut butter." Much to her shame, her stomach started to growl, and Bain smirked.

"I remember that feeling all too well," he said.

"What feeling?" She couldn't help but snap out the question. After everything that she had been through today, she was really struggling to keep up with what was going on.

Her life had gone from panic to fear, to possible death.

She'd gladly worry about keeping a job than worry about being alive by tomorrow.

"Starvation. It's a feeling I know very well."

"You've starved?" she asked. The man didn't look undernourished in the least.

"It was part of being disciplined. I wasn't allowed food until I had earned that right." He put the sandwiches on paper towels. She gasped as he pulled out a knife and cut the rope holding her hands together. "Eat." He pocketed the knife and sat opposite her. She was still trapped to the chair with no way of escaping. He simply watched her as he ate, and she wondered what he was thinking.

She took the sandwich and had a bite. "You were starved? Was this in the army?"

He scoffed. "No. I wasn't trained by no army. I was trained by a bunch of sadistic bastards when I was a kid. Everything had to be earned, and no matter how much we were desperate for food or water, we had to learn to go without. It was a hard life."

Scarlett stared at him, unable to believe that something like that could happen. "Why are you telling me this?"

"Let's be real, Scarlett, you're going to die. I'm just waiting to see if there's someone else I have to end. Now we can make your final hours pleasant, or bad. It's entirely up to you."

She swallowed past the lump in her throat. It had been an awful life now that she thought about it. Boyfriends had been cruel, downright hurtful, and abusive. On top of that, she had parents that didn't love her and a job that stole her ideas. Yeah, she could see an end coming, and it was strange that she actually looked forward to it.

*No!*

She didn't want to die. She wanted to live.

Everything that she had been through in the past thirty-six years were starting to get to her, and she couldn't stand it.

Taking another bite of her sandwich, she refused to give in and give up. She was a lot stronger than this and would fight this feeling that was consuming her.

"Now would you look at that," Bain said, smirking. "There's a fighter inside you after all. I was starting to wonder where your backbone had gone."

"Fuck off." She glared at him, prepared to fight him.

"I'm not going anywhere, babe, and right now, you're turning me the fuck on."

She hadn't expected that, especially as he grabbed his dick, which was easily seen pressed against his pants.

This was insane. She didn't want to notice his large length. The thing was, Bain didn't even reach out to touch her. He released his cock, and then continued to eat his sandwich as if nothing was going on. She watched him, somewhat surprised.

"If you're thinking I'm going to rape you, you're wrong. I won't hurt you."

"You're just going to kill me?"

"Exactly, nothing wrong with that. I'm being honest." He shrugged. "If you entertain me I may keep you around a little longer."

Her blood went cold. She had to have hope that she'd get through this.

Maybe, if she got out of here alive, he'd be a better story than Alexei Semenov.

\*\*\*\*

Bain had fucked up in a big way. He knew that, and so far Boss didn't know that, and he didn't know why he cared. Actually, scrap that, he did know why he cared. Viper had been the one to actually give a good report on him. Killing was what he was known for, and Viper had his back. They had both been in that shithole they had called home as a child. Bain didn't even know how else to describe it.

Staring at the sexy little reporter, he knew her mind was working. If she couldn't have Alexei Semenov, then why not him, the hitman? His story would totally fuck people's heads up, and he was used to that shit.

Right now, he didn't *want* to kill her. Not just because of the fact he could guarantee there was someone out there that knew about her but also because he liked looking at her. The monster inside him seemed to calm. He'd seen the alarm in her eyes when he grabbed his dick, and even though he was hard, he wasn't going to force himself on her. He had a great deal of control. Nothing made him do shit that he didn't want to do. His dick was his own and had been since he killed the people who made him do shit he didn't want to do.

She finished the sandwich, and he went to make another. Killing always worked up an appetite inside him, and he didn't trust anyone to make his food, so sandwiches were the only way to go. The kitchen was fully furnished with all the updated equipment, but he hadn't taken the time to figure out how to cook. He was able to heat up noodles, and that was as far as he was willing to go. Fruit, chocolate, candy, and sandwiches were what he lived on for the most part.

"Have you always killed people for a living?"

There was his little reporter shining through. He smiled and nodded his head. "Yes, I have. It's something

I've been trained to do from a young age."

Her face paled. "How young?"

"Young enough to forget the parents that maybe loved me or not. I don't know. I was taken from the street where I lived. I have a vague memory actually. I was around ten, I'm not sure. I don't even have a clue how old I am." He shrugged. "I've been fine with that. I just made my age up, and that's what I go by."

Her long, brown hair had come out of the bun that it had been held in. He watched as she ran her fingers through the long length. The glossy color looked smooth as silk. Her green eyes never once left him as she watched. He handed her another sandwich. Talking to her was kind of fun, even if totally out of character for him. Bain already knew that Boss was probably going through every single inch of Alexei Semenov place to see who had screamed "help me". His life was going to get fucked up fast, but first, he just enjoyed talking to her.

Bain was a cold, hard killer who had taken out countless men and women over the years, and before that, children. He cut those memories off though because he couldn't handle looking back that far. His life began the moment he was free and when he'd killed all those people that had trapped him.

"I can see you've got a lot of questions, and for some strange and bizarre reason, I actually want to talk to you. I know, it's a shock, but I'm going to keep you alive long enough to tell my story. You better hope by the time that I'm finished that I like you enough."

She was biting into her sandwich, her gaze not wavering, and then his cell phone buzzed. He continued to eat, watching her.

"Can I bargain with you?" she asked.

"Depends what you want to bargain with?" He glanced down at her curves and knew without a doubt that she would be a perfect fit against him. The problem with that was he'd never take a woman's body as a bargaining chip. He'd been forced to do that in the past, listen to women scream as he did what needed to be done to survive.

Over the past twenty plus years since his escape, he'd trawled the streets at night for something to do. Many times he'd passed a random alley to hear a woman beg for a guy to stop. Bain made them stop. There were some men he killed on the spot, especially if they reminded him of someone from his past.

"I want to hear what you've got to say. I can see that you really want to tell me. I've got nothing else to offer you."

"You don't give yourself enough credit. You've got a body there that is pure heaven, but you know what, let's talk about talking. I like that. I think there is someone I'd love to tell my story to, and you're just the person."

She licked her lips, and he saw that he'd unnerved her. *Good.* He didn't want her to think that for a second this was going to be a piece of cake. It wasn't. His life story wasn't easy, and no one would want to hear this.

It was strange because he also wanted to know about her. "Are you sure you don't have a husband?" he asked.

"I'm very sure. I haven't been in a serious relationship for a long time."

"How come?" he asked.

"Wow, you're a nosy person."

He shrugged. "We're passing the time here, babe. You tell me shit, I tell you shit."

She took another bite of her sandwich. "My last boyfriend decided that a woman's place was in the kitchen and cleaning his home, and if something was out of place, he'd make me learn by using his fists."

Bain didn't like hearing that and watched as she stared past his shoulder, not really looking at him.

"It was a difficult time, and finally, something happened and it was the last straw."

"What happened?"

"I don't know you enough to tell you my life story."

His cell phone started to ring again, and he glanced over at it.

"I think you need to get that. It could be important."

Bain reached out and took the call.

"She works for the media? Are you fucking for real? You didn't read the fucking security detail plans?"

Bain all but yelled down the phone. "I've been watching his ass for two weeks straight, and nothing was out of place."

"I don't give a fuck if you'd been standing by his side as part of his detail for the past six years. At Killer of Kings you always expect the unexpected, and this Scarlett woman is an extra fucking detail."

"Don't worry, she won't be a problem."

"I already know that you've got her, Bain. I thought you were supposed to be a professional."

"Fuck you, bastard. You came to me, remember that."

"I came to you because you're damn skilled at what you do, and Viper put in a good word for you. Killer of Kings doesn't do sloppy. Get rid of your problem and handle it."

The call disconnected, and Bain stared at the cell phone. This was one of the reasons he didn't do this shit for real.

"Is everything okay?" Scarlett asked.

He nodded and turned toward her. "Just a problem at work."

Taking a seat opposite her, he stared at her.

She finished off her sandwich, and then her hands rested on her thighs. The rope was tightly wrapped around her waist, securing her to the chair.

He couldn't trust her, and now he was tired. Bending down beside her, he wrapped his arms around her waist and began to unravel the rope.

"What are you doing?" she asked.

"I need a shower, and I'm not going to leave you here." He released her bonds, and then helped her to stand up, brushing the crumbs down her body.

Taking hold of her hand, he started to move up to the next floor to his bedroom, which also had an en-suite bathroom. He grabbed a wooden chair, placed her in it and tied her up once again.

"Seriously? You're going to take a shower while I'm here?"

He took a step back and removed his shirt. Her gaze traveled down his chest, taking in every single piece of ink he'd had decorated on his body. "You like what you see?" he asked.

The ink he'd used to cover up every single scar he'd gained as a child. Only Viper understood what he'd gone through. It was strange this connection he had to the other man. Together they had come out of their nightmare, and yet it had never really left them. There were still moments when Bain woke up sure that he was about to wake up to a stick slammed across his back.

Shaking off the feeling, he removed his pants and boxer briefs until he was fully naked. His cock was long, hard, and there was already pre-cum at the tip, but like so many times he ignored it.

Glancing over at Scarlett he saw that she had

averted her gaze. Running himself a bath, he made sure there were lots of relaxing bubbles. He was getting older, and with his age there were a few aches and pains he had to take care of.

A nice long bubble bath was one of the few luxuries in life that he allowed himself, and right now, he needed to relax. He already felt the beginnings of a migraine, and within an hour he'd be useless as the pain took over.

It was kind of funny, or at least to him it was. He was a hardened killer that was often brought to his knees by the pounding inside his head.

"Do you want a bath?" he asked, looking toward her. She was now staring at him. "I don't mind you having the water after me, but I'll be here as you wash. I'll see you naked."

He watched as she swallowed, her hands rubbing against her thighs.

"I would like a bath, please," she said.

See, he wasn't a total monster.

## Chapter Three

She'd only had sex with two different men in her life, both assholes, but neither of them looked like Bain. His body resembled a sculpture chiseled out of marble, hard and cut. His cock would give any man penis-envy. She tried not to stare, but he was so brazen and confident and very nice to look at. Her chair was poised right outside the open bathroom door, so she could see everything from his tight ass to the trail of hair leading to that monster cock. His body was a living canvas with tattoos all the way down his arms and torso. She supposed she could look away, but she didn't want to.

For a killer, it surprised her when he began adding scented bubbles to his bath. Bain's bathroom had an original claw-foot tub. She'd always liked antiques over modern décor. Once he stepped in, he groaned and sank into the water. He was so big, he barely fit his body into the cramped space.

This house reminded her of her grandmother's old place with the decorative crown moldings and hot water radiators. Scarlett had spent a lot of time at her grandmother's home until she died. Those were some of her best childhood memories. And it was a long time ago.

"This is good stuff, Scarlett."

It was odd how this murderer seemed so personable. He must be a sociopath. He had spoken with Alexei briefly in Russian before casually pulling the trigger—no warning, no emotion. She hoped he didn't do the same to her without notice. Maybe next time he fed her, she'd die with a sandwich in her mouth and bullet in the head.

"You speak English well," she said.

"Why wouldn't I? It's my first language."

"But the Russian. It sounded native."

He chuckled, rubbing the suds over his strong arm up to his shoulder. "I speak a lot of languages. At least six that I can think of offhand. It's necessary in my line of work, something we were taught."

"By those same men who starved you?"

"Exactly, so you can imagine I got the dialects down pat fast."

She only knew English. Learning new things took time and money, both things she didn't have in abundance. Now she'd never get a chance to do any of the things on her bucket list. Scarlett wiggled in her seat to test the bonds, but they were secure, even digging into her waist. It would be the perfect time to escape, but she'd have a real opportunity soon enough. When he'd offered her his dirty bathwater, she'd only agreed because it meant he'd have to untie her.

"Do you live here alone?" she asked.

"Just me. That's how I like it."

She copied his earlier questions. "No wife? Kids?"

The water sloshed as he shifted positions, but she could still only see his shoulders and the back of his head. "Hell no. Family would be a complication. I hate complications."

How could anyone not crave a family, stability, the all-American dream? Didn't everyone want the white picket fence? Even after what she'd been through in relationships, she still dreamed of that elusive happily ever after. Some days that hope, even if unrealistic, was all that kept her going.

Bain must be lonely. He wasn't young. He was mature and weathered—all man. Her thoughts began to drift into uncomfortable territory. His shoulders were broad and corded with muscle, his intricate tattoos trying to reveal his secrets. What stories would they tell?

*What is wrong with me?*

He was her enemy, the man who would probably murder her, not her knight in shining armor. She'd always had the worst taste in men. Now that she was old enough to think objectively, Scarlett blamed a lot of her poor decision making on her deadbeat father. Desperate for acceptance, part of her forever tried to gain his approval through the eyes of men,. It was the only reason she could be attracted to Bain, thriving off his compliments and yearning for his affection. She knew it was wrong and twisted, but she couldn't help herself. Maybe he'd see something special in her, unlike his other victims, unlike Alexei Semenov.

"So you'll just stay by yourself forever? That sounds lonely." Scarlett tried to convince herself she was just calming the beast, befriending her captor so he'd have pity on her. But that was a lie. Bain interested her— the reporter, the victim … the woman.

*"You're* not married," he said.

"That's not by choice. My past relationship didn't exactly work out according to plan."

"If you're so worried about being lonely, why didn't you make it work?"

Scarlett didn't want to talk anymore. She felt her body stiffening, closing from the inside out. It was easy to block out the past, but it was always there, eating away at her. Soon there'd be nothing left.

Bain turned around and looked at her. "I thought you wanted to talk?"

"Not anymore." She refused to look him in the eye.

"Soft spot?"

"Whatever," she said.

"Yeah, that's why I like to be alone. People

always disappoint. The only person I trust is myself." He rolled out his shoulders and settled back into the tub. "Now, tell me why you didn't make it work."

She narrowed her eyes, even though he couldn't see her. "I said I'm done talking."

"Actually, you're not. We had an agreement, you and I. You know the consequences if you piss me off."

Tears stung her eyes. He couldn't make her talk about herself. Then again, if she wanted to live she had to humor him. She could lie, give a good story to appease him, but she was all about the truth. It was why she became a reporter in the first place. She started by helping families being taken advantage of by unethical landlords and women struggling to recoup child support from absentee fathers. She wanted to make the world a better place.

"I told you why I didn't make it work. My last boyfriend was abusive. I couldn't live like that," she said.

"But you wouldn't be lonely."

She shook her head. "There are things worse than being lonely."

He ran his hands over his scalp, the short buzz cut making a scraping sound. "Exactly my point."

Was he referring to the men who'd abused him? "You said you wanted to tell your story. What's your reason for living here alone?"

"If you're talking about a woman, it's not possible for me." He rose to his feet, the water rushing down his hard, muscled frame as he stood. This time his back was to her, each muscle hard and defined. He reached for a towel, first drying his face, then wrapping it securely around his lower half. She studied the artwork on his torso as he moved. "I was one of the oldest boys in the compound, and because of my looks, they trained me to seduce women. It's all a blur now, the fucking, the killing. I really don't want to remember those days."

"I don't understand," she said.

"You asked why I'm alone." He walked into his bedroom. Bain twirled her chair around, with her still securely on it, as he left the en-suite. "That's why. I was forced to be with so many different women for so many fucking years that it numbed me. Emotions, love, everything—it's all gone. Why would I choose to be with a woman now? I just need to be left alone."

"People can change, recover from unspeakable horrors. I've seen it. I know it's possible."

He put on black boxer briefs that hugged his hard ass and strong legs. Scarlett watched him walk about the room from the closet to the dresser. He finally tugged on a pair of navy jogging pants but didn't put on a shirt. She tried not to be too obvious as she snuck in peeks of him. Would he be as hard as he looked? Bain settled on the corner of his king-sized bed, staring at her with such intensity that her words caught in her throat.

"You have no idea the horrors I've lived, sweetheart. I promise whatever you've been through is a cake walk compared to my shit life."

"There's good left in everyone," she whispered. Scarlett wouldn't let him drag her down. She'd been fighting depression for too many damn years. She was barely a shell of woman, fragile and empty. She wanted to think positive, to improve herself and move upward—and she firmly believed Bain could do the same.

He smiled, but it didn't reach his eyes. "Those bastards said I was handsome, irresistible to women. That's why they used me." Bain stood and approached her, grabbed the edge of her chair and dragged it back to his bed. He sat back down on his mattress, only a breath between them now. "All that's changed now," he said.

"What do you mean?"

Bain took her wrist and placed her palm on his chest. His skin was so firm and warm, her pussy throbbing from just that one touch. "Feel me. Really feel me."

She wasn't sure what point he was making until she began to smooth her fingertips over his chest, his shoulders, and then his face. With a gentle caress, she traced all the ridges of old scars she hadn't really noticed until now. He was covered in them. To say she was shocked would be an understatement.

"Not so handsome anymore, eh? I try to hide this shit with ink, but it's not the physical scars that bother me the most. They've fucked up my head so bad that killing's the only thing that keeps me sane."

She swallowed hard. "I think you're perfect." The words slipped from her lips before she really thought better. It wasn't a lie. Bain was the roughest, scariest man she'd ever seen, but also irresistible and hardcore in a way that made her body light up for the first time in her life.

Her hand was still on his cheek, his rough stubble tickling her fingers. She noticed the thick scars under his eye, and she was tempted to kiss it better.

Whatever she thought they'd shared—a moment, a breakthrough—was gone when he bolted to his feet as if her touch scorched him.

He paced back and forth, his chest heaving as if he'd just run a two-minute mile. What had she said to upset him? Had she pegged him wrong? Was he ready to kill? Maybe he was about to prove her wrong once again, just as Jerry and Michael had. She didn't want to believe it, but maybe some people were beyond redemption.

\*\*\*\*

He'd fucked up. Bain knew he shouldn't have brought the witness home with him. He should have just killed her off site and dumped the body. It didn't matter if she disappeared, as long as it didn't lead back to him. All his efforts had been for the benefit of Killer of Kings—he refused to look like an unprofessional. Bain wasn't sure why Boss's opinion mattered so much. It shouldn't.

Now this girl was pushing his buttons, testing him, making him feel things he shouldn't. Boss had made it clear she had to die. He expected Bain to follow through and clean up the potential shit storm that could develop from taking a hostage. But he wasn't ready to follow that order. In fact, he didn't like orders at all. It's the main reason he worked for himself all these years, taking solo contracts, but never committing to anything long term. He couldn't stand being smothered, having any human lord over him.

"Your turn," he said. Bain needed to move onto something new. He desperately needed a distraction from his traitorous thoughts. And his fucking migraine was growing in intensity, messing with his head.

"For what?"

"The bath," he said. "You wanted to go after me, right? The longer you wait the colder the water gets."

She frowned. "Fine."

He squatted down next to her chair and began to undo the tight knots. She rested her hand on his shoulder, but he shrugged her off. No more touching. "Okay, you have ten minutes." He dropped the ropes to the ground.

When his phone started ringing downstairs in the kitchen, he ignored it. He knew it was information on his next hit, even though he'd asked for a text, but Boss would have to wait.

"You can go get that," she said, standing up. "I'd rather undress in private anyway."

"Yeah, not going to happen. I wasn't born yesterday." He sat down on her chair, his legs splayed as he rested his elbows on his knees. "Get undressed. I already told you I'd see you naked."

"Well, I'm shy."

Bain wasn't going to lie, he was disappointed. He'd been looking forward to getting an eyeful of Scarlett's lush curves. His cock was already firm just thinking of them. But he wasn't going to force her to strip if she refused. "Then you'll go without bathing," he said.

With his mood soured, he ordered her out of his room and down the staircase as he followed right behind her. Once in the kitchen, he pointed to her chair as he grabbed his cell off the table.

"Do you still want me to interview you?" she asked.

"Story time's over." He'd been a fool to entertain Scarlett. She'd be his fucking undoing if he continued to play her games.

He called Boss back. "You have the information?"

"You deal with the problem?"

Bain growled, grinding his teeth together rather than speaking.

"Is that a yes?" Boss asked.

"I don't repeat myself. I said it would be handled."

There was a brief silence.

"I'll text you the address and details. This mark needs to take a dive off one of the balconies at lunch hour tomorrow. We need a street full of witnesses for his suicide. Can you handle that?"

"Wire the payment," said Bain. "I'll call you when it's complete."

He turned off the phone before Boss could add any smartass comment about doing things right or not fucking up again. A lecture was the last thing he wanted to hear right now. Bain took a cleansing breath and set his phone back down.

The chair was empty.

*Are you fucking kidding me?* The little reporter moved fast. Too bad her escape attempt was in vain. His house was more secure than Fort Knox, so there was no getting out without his security code. He checked around the main floor, not finding her. The house wasn't huge, so there were only so many places she could hide. It was fucking late, and he needed to get some sleep in preparation for his hit tomorrow. He'd have to be up early and plan out his strategy since he'd been given less than twenty-four hours prep time.

He ran back upstairs, taking the steps two at a time. His bedroom still had the fragrant scent of the bath water. She was nowhere to be found, which meant she could only be one other place—the basement. He hated going down there.

After reaching the door leading to the lower level, he flicked on the light for the lone bulb. It hardly cast any light, creating eerie shadows against the walls. He took the steps slowly, cautiously. Scarlett was feisty, so he didn't trust her not to blindside him with a pipe or crowbar. There was a lot of old shit stored in the basement when he'd bought the house, but he couldn't bring himself to clear it out.

"I know you're down here, sweetheart. I'm really not in the mood, so make it easier for yourself and stop playing games."

No response.

"If I have to climb these stairs without you, I'll lock the fucking door and let you starve to death. It won't be fast, and it won't be pleasant. Is that what you want?"

The sound of an empty Mason jar tipping over caught his attention. She was behind the furnace. Bain cracked his knuckles as he stalked closer. When he neared, she darted out the other side and ran for the stairs. As she tried to crawl up on her hands and knees, he caught her around the waist, tugging her back down and trapping her against the wall with his body. Bain held both her wrists down at her sides.

"Let me go!" she screamed. He gave her credit for struggling like a wild woman. It took a bit of effort to secure her thrashing body.

"Maybe if you hadn't worn a skirt you would have made it up the stairs, but that's as far as you would have gotten."

"Get off me!"

"Settle down," he said. "If you don't stop I'll tie you back to the chair and leave you here." His head was fucking pounding. He released her wrist to rub the back of his neck, and she used the opportunity to pound her little fist against his bare chest.

"That all you got?"

They began to struggle again, and she managed to get up the stairs this time. Why was he even humoring her? He stopped to pick up one of his Glocks from the kitchen, and then caught her in the hallway, grabbing one arm in a firm hold.

"Hit me! I don't care," she shouted, her eyes filled with tears.

"How about I put a bullet in your head instead, like I should have when I found you?"

Her struggle suddenly ceased when he aimed the gun at her temple, the power in her arms going limp as if her fire had been doused. "Do it," she whispered. "Maybe you'll be doing me a favor."

Her green eyes were so big and child-like even though she was very much a woman. She intrigued him. It was the way she'd said her last words. Her tone had changed, as if she'd lost her very soul. "You want to die now?"

"I've been to hell and back already. I'm well aware there are things worse than death."

He released his breath. She had secrets of her own, but he'd let her keep them for now. When he didn't feel like shit, he'd get her to confess it all.

"Well, it's your lucky day because I can't kill you yet." He pointed to the staircase going up, and this time she followed his order. "I have to be sure no one knew you were at Semenov's place. I can't have any more loose ends. Since I have a job tomorrow, I'll be taking you with me. You've shown you can't be trusted."

"You can't earn my loyalty by kidnapping me."

He closed his bedroom door behind them. "Get on the bed," he said.

"What?"

"The bed. Get on it. It's past fucking midnight, and I have to be up early."

She walked backward, not taking her eyes off him. If he'd wanted to, he could have beat the shit out her, raped her, and killed her a dozen different ways. The fact she still had a look of fear in her eyes was starting to piss him off.

The light hurt his head, so as soon as she sat on the bed, he turned off all the lights. Only a faint glow from the moon filtered in through the window. He didn't have curtains on the second-floor rooms. Bain couldn't even count the number of nights he'd lie awake on his bed, staring up at the moon, feeling nothing and everything at the same time. He was fucked up, and there was no way to undo the damage. He was waste of breath. When he died, he'd leave nothing behind, not even a legacy or heir … just death.

He tossed his joggers and slipped under the

blankets.

She looked stiff and uncomfortable. "You going to sleep in your fancy little suit?"

"I'm fine," she said.

"Suit yourself."

He rolled to his back, draping an arm over his eyes as he let out a low groan. It would be simple to take a couple pills to ease the agony, but he didn't trust any kind of painkiller. After being drugged, beaten, and starved when he was young, he never wanted to allow anything to alter his mind again.

The room was quiet enough to hear a pin drop.

He listened to Scarlett breathing next to him, her weight shifting slightly when she moved.

"Are you okay?" she asked.

"What do you mean?"

"You're in pain. I can tell. What's wrong?"

He shook his head to dismiss her. "It's just a headache. I get them all the time."

"Really?" She sat up in the bed, wiggling closer until she was on her knees. When her hand touched his face, he flinched. "Shhh," she cooed, massaging his temples in a rhythmic pattern.

He didn't stop her.

"My grandmother used to do this to me when I had a headache." Her hands worked some kind of magic, soothing the ache and making him feel human again. "I guess it's an old family secret passed down to me. I never tried in on someone else before."

"Why're you doing this for me?" he asked. Bain seized her hand and hoisted himself up into a sitting position.

She didn't answer him. They looked at each other, and that same fucking feeling he had earlier came back. This time he wasn't as strong. He cupped the back of her head and pulled her closer. He paused briefly, then kissed her hard on the mouth. What he didn't expect was the way her lips melted against his with no resistance at all.

## Chapter Four

This was the craziest thing she had ever done in her life. Scarlett knew that there was no way out for her. Even if she went to the cops and begged for protection they couldn't help her. No one could. In the few hours she had come to know Bain, she'd learned he wasn't a man to be messed with. He always found his target.

The feel of his lips on hers was such a heady experience, and she closed her eyes, simply basking in his touch. He cupped the back of her head, and his tongue stroked along her lips before diving in.

She whimpered as he held her close. For the first time in her life she felt small, delicate, and her body came to life, wanting so much more. Resting her hand on his chest, she felt the pounding of his heart and suddenly pulled away, staring at him.

There was no way this man was human. He seemed so cold, so callous. How did he even feel? And yet, his heart was pounding, and she'd seen the pain in his eyes.

"Why wouldn't I do it for you?" she said. "You were hurting, and I'm not a cruel person. You don't deserve to suffer." She dropped her hand down on the bed and licked her suddenly sore lips. It had been a long time since she had been kissed like that.

Bain didn't let go of her head, and she couldn't look in his eyes anymore. It was just too hard to have these feelings rushing through her. Nothing made a whole lot of sense.

"I've never been very good at any of this," she said.

"What do you mean?"

"Sex. Coping. Understanding. You wouldn't

understand. I've never been able to connect, and the men I've been with, they weren't exactly good guys." He released her head, and she ran a hand over her face and wrinkled her nose. She stank really bad. "My last boyfriend, it was bad, and I finally left him over a year ago. Ever since I was a little girl, I always wanted to be a reporter. One thing after another stopped me from being what I wanted to be. Then this opportunity opened up, but again, if you don't fit the model, they pass you over. I'm not some twenty-something anymore. I'm not slim, not that I ever was, and I'm not pretty. I'm fat, frumpy, and ugly, trying to make my way in this superficial world. This interview was going to kickstart it." She smiled at him. "I know you don't want me to interview you. You're just waiting to find out knows about where I was." She took a deep breath. All of her life she had fought these feelings of not belonging. Only her grandma had ever been able to make her feel wanted, loved. Death would be easier. "I told someone. I don't want you to hurt her."

"I already know you told someone, Scarlett."

"You're a killer. Contracted and all of that. Kill me, put me in my apartment. You can make it look like an accident or something. I've got a history of depression." She saw him frown. "Please, don't hurt her."

She saw his jaw clench. "You're begging me to kill you?"

"Yes. Kill me, Bain. No one has to die because of me."

"You have a history of depression?"

"Yes. See? I have the perfect out, and you don't even have to work hard for it. I won't fight you." He suddenly pulled away and began to pace beside his bed, and he glared at her. "You know it's the only way." She couldn't believe that she was begging for someone to kill her. Tears filled her eyes, and she climbed off the bed.

"Please."

"I'm not going to kill you."

"Why not?"

"I want to tell my story. I wasn't lying to you about that, and I'm not ready to kill you." He took hold of her hand and turned it over. "You have no previous scar wounds."

"I was depressed, not suicidal. I've not tried to end my life before. Never thought I had the guts to do it." She shrugged and frowned. "It's weird how I'm feeling right now. I've never felt like this." She placed a hand over her lips and stared at him. She didn't like the sadness in his eyes as he looked at her.

"I'm not going to kill you, Scarlett. Now, do you want to bathe? There will be plenty of hot water." He tugged back on his joggers and flicked on a lamp.

She crossed her arms over her chest. Did she want to wash? Yes, she did. She smelled and not in a very nice way. "I won't run away."

"I know you won't. There's nowhere for you to run. This place is heavily guarded. I'm not going to hurt you." He brushed past her going straight toward the bathroom.

Even though this man held her life in his hands, she couldn't help but admire his ass. It was so tight as he walked. The sweats he wore molded to his ass, and then went baggy around the thighs.

He paused and turned toward her. "Are you coming?"

"You're not killing me?"

"I said I wasn't killing you. You're easy to talk to." He shook his head. "You're fucking confusing me. Just get your ass in the bathroom."

She stared around the bedroom and wondered what the hell was going on. One moment he wanted to go to bed to sleep, now he wanted her to wash. Nothing made any sense, and tonight was totally illogical.

Entering the bathroom, she saw him bending over the bath, adding some scented bubbles.

Scarlett smiled. "I never imagined you having bubbles in the bath."

"This one offers to relax muscles, and I need to relax these tired muscles as much as I can. I'm not getting any younger." He stood tall, and she heard his back click, at which she winced. "I'm no spring chicken anymore."

"I know that feeling all too well."

"I'll be at the door. I'll give you enough privacy to get in the bath so I don't see anything."

She watched as his back was to her, and then she removed her dirtied white blouse, followed by her skirt. As soon as she was naked and in the bath, she let him know. He took a seat and leaned back, arms folded over his chest.

"How is your head?"

"It's fine. Whatever you did, it eased the pressure, and I can think now."

"I'm glad I was able to help. Migraines can be the worst." She ran her hands through the bubbles. Everything was somewhat surreal to her. "Do you have any family?" she asked.

"No. None. I would say in the entire world I have one friend, and I think 'friend' is even pushing that description. We're colleagues." He ran a hand over his head. "We were captured, and he was one of the hardest people I've ever known. Some of the kids the people took off the street, they were lambs heading to the slaughter. They didn't make it a couple of days, let alone weeks. His name's Viper."

She nodded. "And he was a child soldier of some kind? Like you?"

"You could say that. We were given jobs even at a young age to prove our loyalty. The moment they took us, any sense of a childhood was destroyed. There was no time for playing around or games. There was no Christmas or birthday parties. It was work, training, practice. Over and over again. Everything else faded away."

He was opening up to her, and she found his voice soothing. It was hard and gruff and hypnotic at the same time. Licking her dry lips, she turned so that she was facing him. The bubbles gave her some semblance of modesty.

"What happened to the kids who couldn't do it?" she asked.

The pain in his eyes along with the disgust cut her to the core. "Their bodies mounted up until they burned them. If you couldn't do what they wanted, you weren't good enough to keep around, and if you weren't good enough to keep around, you were only useful for one thing, and that was training."

She covered her mouth as she watched a single tear slide out of the corner of his eye, and he moved fast, wiping it away as if it was never there. Sucking her lips into her mouth, she closed her eyes and couldn't even begin to imagine.

"It's like something out of a horror film," she said.

"To a lot of people it probably is. It was no picnic. My story doesn't end with a happily ever after, Scarlett, but for a lot of kids, it ended in pain, suffering, and death. Those assholes didn't give a shit about anyone or anything."

"Killing has become your life's work."

"It's all I know, and it will always be what I know." He pointed at his ink. "You think I didn't fight for them? That I didn't take beatings every single day to try and save them? None of our captors would listen. Some of the kids were no older than five, and they had no right to be there."

"What about their families?" she asked. "There had to have been searches. People don't just allow kids to be taken."

"They don't allow kids from good families to be taken, Scarlett. The world isn't full of good people. Kids come and go, and no one gives a shit unless their parents do."

The thought of those kids, alone and dying, broke her heart. "How old were you?"

He stared at her for the longest time, and with each second of silence her heart broke. "I was around ten years old. I was one of the first kids they took. We're done talking tonight. I need you to finish washing." He stood up, walking away. She looked at the vacant chair, and her heart broke for the boy he had once been. He was the oldest boy, and yet he'd been taken at such a young age.

"Bain?" She called his name, needing an answer to her question. He appeared in the doorway holding a pair of boxers and a really long shirt. "What happened to the people that took you?"

"They're dead. Viper and I, together we made sure they were fucking annihilated."

"Good." And she meant that, deep in her soul. She was pleased those evil bastards were dead.

She finished washing her body and her hair in the scented soap. When she was done, Bain held out a towel. She stood up and took it.

"I thought you said you were shy."

"I lied."

\*\*\*\*

The following day, Bain stood in the center of the apartment, keeping a safe distance away from the balconies. Lunch hour was fast approaching, and he'd already opened the door. This wasn't the first time he'd thrown someone off a balcony, and it wouldn't be the last. The furniture in the apartment was modern, black leather and abstract art. Not his style.

Sucking on his lollipop, he checked the time to see that he still had five minutes before the mark came walking through the front door.

There were going to be plenty of witnesses to the death, which was exactly what Boss wanted. Bain's thoughts were not on the easy mark though. They were on the woman he'd stored in the trunk of his car after giving her a sedative. He could have left her home, but he couldn't risk her causing a problem. He liked his place, and he couldn't stand mess. She'd probably trash the whole house.

He didn't trust Boss either.

Bain wasn't an idiot and figured Boss would find a way into his house and deal with Scarlett himself. People thought Bain was a cold and ruthless bastard, and yet they didn't have a clue who Boss was. That man was a cold fucker. He'd stab you in the heart while laughing at one of your jokes. Even Bain was cautious around the owner of Killer of Kings.

The moment he thought about Scarlett, the image of her naked with bubbles running down her body filled his mind. She was sexy as fuck. Her curves were meant for a man's loving. Her hips were wide and her ass plump. He didn't know what he loved most, those big breasts with the large red nipples, or her thighs, which he could imagine wrapped around his waist as he fucked her hard.

She was the first woman that had ever affected

him this way. He was trained in all kinds of seduction, taking women to new heights. When he was younger he was shown how to please a woman in every way. He'd been forced to practice on so many different women. Their faces had all blended together until he got no enjoyment from it at all. All pussy was the same. It was either tight or loose.

Since becoming a man, he'd taken plenty of women, but it had been on his own terms. Scarlett was different. Her lips last night had awakened him in some way, and a little part of him was freaking out.

One kiss from her, and his night had been filled with thoughts that an average teenage boy should be plagued with, not him.

He was past wet dreams and shit like that. When he'd woken up this morning, she had been wrapped in his arms, and his cock had been too fucking hard to deal with, the tip wet from his pre-cum. He'd been unable to resist running his hands up and down her glorious body, and yet that hadn't been enough for him. Where was his unbreakable control? He didn't have a clue what was happening to him.

Now he had to focus on the task and put those memories to rest. The sedative he'd given Scarlett before they left would start to wear off soon. He had timed it so that he'd be back at his place by the time she began screaming. *Tick tock.*

His cell phone went off, and he cursed. There were only a couple of minutes left, and he didn't want to lose his element of surprise. Answering the call, he saw it was Boss. "Are you for fucking real right now? I'm on a job, and you think it's the right time to call?"

"I missed you."

He rolled his eyes. "What the fuck do you want?"

"I want to know if you ended your problem. You

need to. If she's reported missing, she becomes a big fucking inconvenience."

Bain rubbed his eyes. "I'm handling it."

"You need to handle it soon. Cops will start looking, especially if her friend lets them know exactly where she was going last night, and there are a lot of dead bodies there. When she's not there, they're going to want to know where the fuck she is. Time's ticking."

He heard the key in the lock.

"I'll handle it." He hung up the phone before Boss could say anything more. The door opened, and the mark was alone, talking on his cell phone.

Everything went according to plan. The guy ended the call, dropped his suitcase off, and then headed toward the balcony, which was when Bain struck. The mark went over the edge, and Bain didn't stay to watch as chaos ensued. Leaving the room, he kept on sucking his lollipop, heading toward the parking garage. He checked to make sure no one was around and opened up the trunk of his car. There she was, safe and sound, still dressed in his clothes. She was going to be so pissed, but he liked her fighting.

He didn't like it when she'd given up last night and begged him to kill her. There was more fire in that sexy body, and he was determined to deal with it.

Climbing behind his wheel, he drove out of the parking lot and headed back home.

His cell phone went off, and he sighed.

"You shoved him off the balcony?" Boss asked. "You could have been seen."

"I'm a fucking ghost. It was a textbook hit. Job done."

"That's why I hired you," said Boss.

Bain hung up the cell, and drove home.

By the time he pulled into his garage, Scarlett was

banging on the roof of the trunk, screaming.

Just thinking of her chest heaving as she yelled and fought him was enough to turn him on. His anger subsided as he opened the trunk.

"You fucking asshole. What the fuck did you give me?" she asked. She was so angry she was even cussing at him. Just hearing the word *fuck* from her voice had his dick getting harder.

"It was just a little sleeping pill. You've been out like a light. I needed to do this job, and I knew if I took you, you'd help the poor fucker that was due to die today."

"You killed someone else?" she asked.

"I did."

"What if he was a good person?"

"He specialized in getting pedophiles out of prison. He was a monster protecting monsters. I did a good deed today."

She closed her eyes and sighed. "I can't handle this right now. My mouth is so dry." He took her hand, and she pushed him away. "I really don't want you touching me right now. I can't believe you drugged me."

"For a good cause."

"Is that what you do? Kill people who are bad?"

He paused. "You don't want me to answer that. Not yet."

"You're right. I really don't want to know any more right now. I feel like I'm going to throw up."

He wrapped his arm around her back and held her close, loving the way she seemed to collapse against him. She needed some food, and as he entered his home and led her to the counter, he opened his fridge.

"Another sandwich?" she asked.

"Do you want takeout? There's a Chinese place that has the most amazing wontons. I love them." He showed her the paper menu he kept in the drawer.

"I'm confused. First I'm not allowed to eat, and now I get a choice? Why are you being nice to me?" she asked.

"Why wouldn't I? I've completed a job, so I'm feeling good." Then he decided to test her reaction to the news Boss gave him. "Just so you know, someone went to the cops saying you didn't make it into work."

He watched as she froze, her gaze panicked as she looked at him.

"Do you want some decent food?" He had no intention of killing her. Boss wouldn't let him get away with it, though. There was no way she would ever be able to rid herself of the mark on her head. Boss would kill her to make sure nothing came back to him as leader of Killer of Kings.

"I would love some food."

He watched the acceptance of her situation take over. She was worried, her mind working a mile a minute.

She tucked some hair behind her ear. "I'll eat anything. I'm pretty easygoing. I love spicy food, sweet and sour, stuff like that."

Bain touched her hand, and she pulled back. "You don't have to be afraid."

"I'm not an idiot, Bain. I know what this means. Just don't kill my friend, okay? With me out of the picture, she may just keep her job."

Bain gritted his teeth. "Do you trust me?"

She tilted her head to the side and shrugged. "I don't really know you."

He tapped his fingers on the edge of the counter. This wasn't right. He didn't want her like this. He had to show her how he felt in the only way he knew how. Grabbing a knife from the set on the far wall, he slit his palm open, then he took her hand, and gave it a similar small nick. He'd done this many years ago with Viper. To him, this was the most sacred oath he'd ever given.

"What the hell are you doing?" she asked, trying to tug her hand away. He waited for her to calm, then carefully matched their scars together, watching for her reaction.

"We're blood now, Scarlett. I won't let anything happen to you. While you're with me, you'll be safe, do you understand?"

"I know you're crazy."

"I haven't shared any of my shit with anyone. You're the first woman I've trusted, and this is not something I take lightly. You need to listen to what I'm telling you, Scarlett." He held her hand firmly in his grip. "When you have nothing to your fucking name, and all you've got to share is blood, it matters. I've only ever done this once, and I'll never do it again. Do you understand?"

She nodded, and tears once again glistened in her eyes.

Just once, he didn't want to make her cry. Was that really too much to ask?

## Chapter Five

She should be completely freaked out. A stranger had mingled their blood together, which would normally terrify her because of all the contagious diseases out there. She'd even prepared news reports on tainted blood, and some of the outcomes were horrifying.

But instead of being scared, or even upset, she felt uniquely special. All her life, she'd wanted to belong to someone, to feel loved and wanted. As crazy as it seemed, Bain had offered her a piece of himself and an odd promise—to not kill her. She'd take it for now, but deep down, she hoped for a lot more. The rules of right and wrong had gone out the window once the bullets started flying at Semenov's. Her world had tilted off its axis ever since Bain had been thrust into her life. There was no going back.

"You know what, I don't want to see you like this. No more tears. Come on," Bain said.

Scarlett narrowed her eyes as he led her to the front door, unsure of what to expect. She watched as he entered the code: 24926 for the exit alarm system.

"Where you taking me?" She followed him to that same black BMW in the garage. A little piece of her was terrified he'd set her free, return her to her previous reality. Maybe a big piece. This hulk of a man was broken on the inside and breathtaking on the outside. The fact he thought she was beautiful already put him high above her previous boyfriends. And he hadn't hurt her. Bain was a murderer, savage and ruthless, yet he'd barely put his hands on her. She kept expecting for it to come— a slap, a punch, an ugly insult. Now she was actually starting to trust him, and ever since last night and the kiss to end all kisses, she wanted him in unspeakable ways.

"You need something proper to wear, and we need food." He opened the passenger door for her. "So we're taking a quick drive into the town."

She frowned. "No trunk?" It had been the only way she'd traveled with Bain, cramped in the tight, dark space. It seemed foreign to be offered a normal seat in the car.

"Don't tempt me."

The leather seats were soft and warm against her thighs. She put on her seatbelt and watched as Bain started up the vehicle, the blue dashboard lights flicking on. He cleaned up nicely. He still had on the full suit he'd worn to kill that pedophile, his biceps bulging as he reached for the steering wheel. She wasn't sure who was worse, Bain for murdering that man or her for being glad it happened. Scarlett realized she would have failed miserably as a field reporter. There was no way she could remain impartial when one person was being victimized. Her skills were in research and intel. She almost envied Bain's lifestyle. He was judge and jury with no fear holding him back from bringing justice to the bad guys. Then again, maybe he'd kill any person if he was paid enough.

"You said you won't kill me," she stated.

"Yeah."

"But you can't let me go?"

The hum of the engine grew louder as he gave the car more gas, the scenery whipping by in her peripheral vision. She held onto the edges of her seat as her heart began to race. Her life had never been a thrill ride like this.

"It's for your own good. Without me, you wouldn't last a day," he said.

"What do you mean? Who would want to kill me? All of Semenov's men are dead, and you destroyed all the security footage."

"My boss doesn't like loose ends. You're a loose end."

She kept quiet. Bain wanted to protect her, and it turned her on to be so important to another human being—to a beast like Bain. Even her own parents discarded her as if she had no worth.

He parked the car on a busy street. It was almost dinner hour, and she was getting hungry.

"I can't go anywhere in public like this." She was still wearing Bain's oversized shirt and boxers. Not a good look for the Junction area of the city.

He squeezed the steering wheel, staring straight ahead. "It would have been better if I'd put you in the trunk, or drugged you."

"Really? I won't leave the car. Like you said, it's dangerous for me anyway, right?"

"Every chance you've gotten, you've tried to get away. I can't trust you," he said.

She pointed to the shop right beside them. "Just get me anything decent to wear—extra large. I like blue and purple, if it matters. You'll be able to see me through the store windows."

He took a deep breath, scanning the crowds as they walked by and darted across the road. "I'm putting the car alarm on, so don't touch the door handle. If you try to get away, I'll be back in less than one fucking minute. I won't be happy if I have to chase you down."

"Relax. I just want food and clothes."

He adjusted a shoulder-holstered gun under the front flap of his suit jacket, and then stepped out of the car. The alarm system beeped three times as it activated. Scarlett watched Bain. He towered over the crowds, and his presence was so menacing that they parted for him as he moved. Just before he entered the little specialty shop, he turned and stared directly at her. God, he did wild things to her body. His musky cologne still lingered in the car, invading all her senses. Why did he have to have so much self-control?

Scarlett was alone. She could run into the crowd, honk the horn, or attract attention. She would have loved this opportunity yesterday. Today, not so much. Her past had been rough, filled with heartache and abuse. There was one secret Bain didn't know. This secret had a life of its own, haunting her, pulling her into a ravenous pit of depression whenever she didn't resist. It was easier said than done to let go of the past and move on. She understood Bain more than he knew. He had his demons, but so did she.

Bain returned in record time, rescuing her from her darkening thoughts. She would have barely started combing through the racks, but he entered the car with two bags, thrusting them onto her lap. "Get dressed."

"Here?"

"The windows are heavily tinted. Just make it quick."

She started sifting through the contents of the bags and found a pair of black capri pants and a purple shirt with three-quarter sleeves. She smiled to herself. Scarlett started wiggling into the capris, lifting her hips to get them on in the cramped passenger seat. Bain had already seen her naked, but there were so many people passing by.

"What next?" she asked, trying to discreetly switch shirts.

"We'll get some food. I think a change of scenery will do you good, no?"

"You're actually taking me out in public? All this change because of the blood thing?"

"I'm trying to be nice. It's not something I usually

do. You want me to stop?"

She shook her head and began twisting her hair up into a bun. Bain reached across the center console and stilled her hand. "Leave it out," he said. "I like it loose."

Her chest felt like it was clenching down around her heart. Was she actually falling for a hitman?

They got out of the car, and she felt awkward walking next to Bain. He was so much taller than she was, a presence unto himself. Not to mention he was completely out of her league. She could already see the way women looked at him, a desperate longing in their eyes. When he didn't respond to their blatant flirting, it pleased her deep down inside.

*If you were smart, Scarlett, you'd run the other way.* Her first serious relationship with Jerry ended because he'd been a serial cheater. He'd torn her confidence to shreds, and made her more needy and clingy than she'd been to start out with. Then came Michael, a few years later. She could never have prepared herself for the physical and mental abuse. It crept in slowly until it became so extreme, so all-encompassing, that dysfunction became her whole world. She felt like nothing, and never believed she deserved better. It was a vicious cycle of abuse, and she'd been caught in it for much too long. Scarlett would probably still have been trapped in that dark world if the unthinkable hadn't happened—but it had.

And it changed her forever.

Now there was Bain. He was just another mistake, a man she should stay far, far away from. She needed to put an end to her fucked up relationships and find a good man, one with a normal job, normal life, normal hopes and dreams, and a normal body. Normal was good, right? Then why couldn't she stop envisioning herself naked in Bain's bed? Why was he taking control of all her thoughts?

He pointed to an outdoor patio on the sidewalk up ahead. "You want to stop there?" he asked.

"Sure."

When his hand settled possessively at the small of her back, she held her breath. Tingles and warmth broke out where he touched her and traveled down between her legs. She expected him to be embarrassed of her. Most men were. Scarlett was happy with who she was, but she wasn't disillusioned about the superficial and highly critical world she lived in. Working with the media put things into everything into perspective—hot guys didn't settle for big girls.

****

Bain hated crowds. He rarely came into the city on his own accord. Walking through the throngs of law-abiding citizens made him feel like a monster. It was the beauty by his side that anchored him. He focused his energy on keeping her safe, ensuring no asshole got into her personal space.

They sat down at a small table at some hippy café. He wanted to impress Scarlett, to be what she needed, even though he knew it would never be enough.

"What if someone sees me?" she asked. Boss had given him the inside scoop about Scarlett, but her friend hadn't reported her missing yet. He still wasn't sure what the fuck he was going to do about the whole situation. This was the first time he had a conscience, or any issue finishing a job. It would be so simple if he could end her, wrap his hands around her throat until her life slipped from her body—but he couldn't do it. Fuck, but he wanted to keep her.

"I'm not worried."

A twenty-something waitress passed them menus. She lingered, and it was blatantly obvious she was trying to get his personal attention. He ignored her until she left. The only thing he knew about women was how to thoroughly pleasure them, and since he'd been forced to do that for so many fucking years, he wanted no part of it. And it pissed him off that she assumed he'd cheat on his date. Just because he was rough around the edges and covered in ink didn't automatically make him a lowlife prick.

"You know what you're getting?" he asked.

She'd kept her head down, her shoulders lowered. Bain knew she wasn't shy, she'd said so herself. He couldn't understand how a woman with so much going for her could lack confidence. Maybe her asshole ex had fucked with her head.

"I think so," she said, folding the menu back on the table.

"You never shut up when we're at my place. What's going on with you?"

She glared at him. "Nothing."

He growled. This was just one of a million reasons he was single. Women infuriated him with their mixed signals. "Was it our waitress?"

When she didn't respond, he knew he was on the right track. "She's a stupid bitch if she thinks I'd choose her over my prize."

Scarlett looked up at him, eye to eye contact without saying a word.

"That's right, babe. I'm talking about you." He reached low and tugged her chair closer, the legs scraping loudly against the concrete patio. "And you're right about the color. The purple looks beautiful on you." He ran the back of one finger along the edge of her jaw. That same desperate urge to kiss her took over, but he controlled it, pushing the need away.

"Thank you," she whispered.

He narrowed his eyes. "You're not comfortable with compliments?"

"I'm just not used to them. They make me suspicious."

Bain chuckled. "I guarantee you, I don't go out of my way to impress anyone. If I give you a compliment, take it."

They ordered their food and received it about twenty minutes later. Bain had a club sandwich.

"I thought you hated sandwiches," said Scarlett.

"Never said that." He finished another bite. "I love them. Anyway, this one's fancy."

"I should make you some real food one day," she said.

"You know how to cook?"

She nodded, taking another spoonful of soup into her mouth. He watched the way her pouty lips wrapped around the utensil, and his cock firmed up in his slacks. After decades of numbness, no desire for love, Scarlett made him feel a powerful longing he'd never felt before.

He wanted to pretend he hadn't just killed a target this afternoon, go to the grocery store with Scarlett, and play house. It was all a fucking illusion, a life not meant for him. Bain was a killer for hire, nothing more. He wouldn't even know how to live a normal life if he tried because he'd never been raised with any values or expectations beyond murder and seduction.

They ate and talked until the streetlights came on. He hadn't realized how late it had gotten, too wrapped up talking with Scarlett. For the first time in a long time, he felt like a whole man, not a broken son of a bitch. "I want to kiss you," he said.

She swallowed hard, the candle on the table reflecting in her big green eyes "Okay…"

"Tell me to stop if you want to."

He didn't care what anyone around them thought, never had given a shit about other people's opinions. Bain tucked her soft curves against him and kissed her lips, losing himself as the kiss quickly became deeper and deeper. It was soft, sweet, and gentle. It felt real, more than a moment of passion. He pulled back, but he'd wanted to keep going, to trail those kisses down her neck. Fuck, he wanted her naked and bent over the table.

Bain was losing it. He paid the bill, then took Scarlett's hand.

"Want to walk for a bit?" he asked. He liked spending time with her, pretending things were different. Once they returned to his house, he'd have to deal with his reality and the complication she was in his life. Boss would only wait so long for him to clean up the mess.

"Okay."

They walked hand in hand. The sky had darkened but the streets still had shoppers, and the night life scene had already started to pick up. Bain didn't drink, and he'd always hated being around people. The only time he'd ever set foot in a bar or club was to carry out a hit. With the drugs, alcohol, and music, they were always the easiest contracts.

"Bain, what happens next?"

"What do you mean?" he asked.

"You're confusing me. First you want me dead, and now you're acting like we're on a date or something. I don't know if I'm coming or going."

What could he tell her? The truth was raw and dirty. He had to find and kill her friend, and then knock Scarlett off and dump her body at one of Semenov's clubs so her death looked related to her interview with the Russian mobster. The longer he was with her, the less likely he'd complete what needed to be done. He'd broken the most important rule drilled into him as a captive—never get personal. Never fall in love.

"Let's just live in the moment," he said. Bain wasn't sure exactly how old he was, but he figured over forty. Was it normal for a man his age to feel his heart race from something simple like holding a pretty girl's hand? It felt more intimate than all the sex he'd had in his life put together.

"Scarlett? Is that you?" A man wearing khakis and a red t-shirt stopped in front on them, and Scarlett's grip on his hand tightened.

"I have nothing to say to you," she said, trying to walk around him. When the guy blocked them from passing, Bain wasn't going to have it.

"Who the fuck is this?" Bain asked, feeling a unique possessiveness wash through him.

Scarlett's demeanour changed, her body and presence closing in on itself. "My ex's brother," she said.

"Really." Bain looked the shit up and down.

"Michael's been trying to contact you for ages. Where've you been staying?"

"I have a restraining order. He shouldn't be trying to find me," she said. "Just stay away from me."

The piece of shit scowled at Scarlett. "He's not going to like this. You've already moved on to another man when he wants to work things out?"

"I left him over a year ago," she said. "He has no say over my life, and he never will again."

Bain could practically feel her nerves, her fear tainting the air. He didn't like it.

"Back the fuck off," Bain said. He glanced around, the streets full of night owls. Too many witnesses for him to put a bullet in this asshole.

He shouldered the guy as he passed, securely holding Scarlett's hand. It was disappointing when he didn't try to pick a fight.

After walking another block away, they approached a small group of rowdy bikers spilling outside one of the popular dive bars. It was time to get Scarlett back to his house. He didn't want her exposed to any more shit tonight. This outing was supposed to be about making her happy, not creating more problems.

"Nice tits, baby!" shouted one of the bikers.

Bain shoved Scarlett behind him and punched the bastard with a clean, straight shot to the face. It was enough to send him toppling backward into his friends. A few others rushed him. The venom in Bain's veins unleashed. He grabbed one in a headlock, punching him into unconsciousness before taking on the other two. It was child's play compared to other scrapes he'd been in. Bain briefly squatted down, pulling out a lethal switchblade from his boot. He played with it so efficiently, he had the rest of the crowd morbidly transfixed.

"Anyone else want to say something to my woman?"

There were no takers, so he backed away and led Scarlett back to his BMW.

"You didn't have to do that," she said once they were clear of any trouble.

"Yeah, I did," he said. "What kind of man stands back while his woman's insulted?"

She looked up at him as they walked. "I'm your woman now?"

He shook his head. "They didn't know that."

"Right…"

He wasn't sure if that sounded like disappointment. There was no way Scarlett wanted anything to do with him. She tolerated him because she was essentially his prisoner. She'd tried to escape every time he turned around, so she wouldn't want to be his woman. She was a good girl, and good girls married nice men—men who put in their nine to five every day and paid their taxes.

He opened the passenger door for her. Once he'd settled inside, the quiet was deafening. "That ex of yours. He the one who hurt you?"

Scarlett nodded. "I've been hiding for a long time. He destroyed my life, and it seems even that's not enough for him."

"Want me to kill him?"

Her mouth fell agape. "You can't just kill anyone because you feel like it," she said. "That's not how real life works … even if we want it to."

"I'll do it for you," he said. "Then you won't have to look over your shoulder."

"So you're letting me go?"

He didn't want to let go, not ever. The thought of being in his house alone again made him feel uneasy. The solitude had always been his strength, but now he wanted to hear Scarlett's chatter, hear her breathing next to him at night, and feel the passion she roused in him effortlessly.

"Not yet."

He pulled onto the road, heading away from the city, back to his sanctuary … or his personal prison. He wasn't so sure anymore.

## Chapter Six

Entering Bain's home again that night, Scarlett was confused, which shouldn't be at all surprising when she thought about how much her life had changed within forty-eight hours. She'd gone from living a really shitty life, to being kidnapped by a man she was having sexual fantasies over. Now she was enjoying the fact he considered her his woman. Her feelings were all over the place.

"I'm sorry," Bain said, which had her turning in the main hall. There had been many times tonight that she could have run away, and yet she hadn't. Not once had she wanted to leave his side. Even though she had watched him kill, she felt safe around him. He would protect her from everything.

"Why are you sorry?"

"I wanted you to have fun tonight."

"I did have fun. It was nice being with you, and not scared." That fact her ex's brother, Neil, turned up was just bad luck. She had a restraining order, and for the past year she'd been able to live her life without fear, and that was the way it was going to stay. Also, in a weird way, it was refreshing knowing that Bain had offered to kill her ex for her. "I was curious, how much do you charge?" she asked.

"What do you mean?"

"You offered to kill my ex. I just wondered how much that would be?"

His laugh didn't offer much comfort. "You couldn't afford me, babe. I offered to do it free of charge."

"How much does a hit cost?" she asked.

"Is this for a story?"

"Nope, this is me being curious about a world I thought was left in movies."

"It differs depending on the person, and who they are. If it's someone important, but it's high risk, it can cost about ten mill. Some of them, like the guy today, can be between five and seven."

"Are you serious?" she asked.

"Do you have a couple of mill lying around the house?"

"No."

"Then I would do it free of charge."

"I actually think you're serious. You are serious?"

"I don't joke around about money. Or killing. Never have, never will."

She was amazed. "Someone would actually pay you that kind of money?"

"And more."

Scarlett didn't know what to say, so she followed him into the sitting room. He collapsed down on the sofa, and she sat down beside him. "Why do you do it?" she asked. So many questions were whirling around her head.

"I've always been good at killing. I told you that."

"Do you think you'll ever do anything else besides killing?"

"No. I'll probably be dead. The thing about being a killer, there's always someone willing to take your place, even take you out."

She bit her lip and leaned back. "Thank you. For defending me today. You didn't have to do that."

"You were with me. I wanted you to have fun, but those assholes ruined it. That guy, is he going to be a problem?"

"Neil? Nah, he shouldn't be."

"He was talking about a guy named Michael."

"The ex I've got a restraining order against. He's

not a very nice man, and he was the final straw. I don't trust men. I don't want anything to do with them." She laughed. "I should just learn to stick with what I know. I thought I was making a fresh start. Becoming a reporter." She blew out a breath. "Have you ever felt so out of your depth before?"

"Not for a long time, but I've felt it. Sometimes it's hard to let go of that kind of feeling." He placed his hand on her knee, and she stared at it. His hand was so large as it rested on her body. The heat from his palm was doing something to her, and she had never felt this hard rush of desire before.

"You said you knew how to seduce a woman. Did it ever mean anything to you?" she asked. "Being with that many women."

"They all blended together, Scarlett. They meant nothing and were simply a means to an end." He began to stroke her knee.

Resting her head in her hands, she tried to think of anything to say to distract herself. "You know, all I've wanted my entire life was for someone to love me, to want to be with me, and to never let me go."

His cold eyes stared back at her. Tears filled her own, and she gazed back down on that tattooed hand on her knee.

"Is it crazy that right now I feel closer to you than I've felt to anyone else in my life?" She returned his gaze once again. The hand made her gasp as it slowly slid up. She couldn't look away from Bain, nor did she want to.

His eyes dropped down to her lips and then back up again.

Was he going to kiss her?

She wanted his lips on hers. The fire burned brighter than anything else in her life.

"You've never had a man devote his time to your

pleasure?"

"No. I've always been a means of them getting what they want. You know, being the fat girl all of my life, it's what I should expect. I've been told that if I lose weight, they may have given me pleasure."

His hand was moving farther up her thigh, and with each inch, she was struggling to think coherent thoughts. He was a killer, a machine, and yet it didn't matter to her. There was something about Bain that called to her. Even as she should be frightened at what they had already shared, she wanted more. She wanted his lips on her, and his hands on her body, consuming her with pleasure.

"You're not fat. I don't think so."

She smiled. "You're being sweet."

"I know what I like, and I happen to think your curves are a blessing." He gripped her hip, and she couldn't help the gasp that fell from her lips. "There is a great deal I like about you, Scarlett, and I barely even know you."

Should she tell him to stop? The grip on her hip tightened, and her eyes closed as her body sparked to life. His lips touched her neck, and she moaned. This was the most touch any man had ever given her. In Bain's arms she felt starved for affection, for touch. She would give anything for him not to stop. The feel of his hands and his arms around her was like an addiction she didn't want to break.

His lips moved from her neck, and she reached out, touching his face as he kissed her. She wasn't afraid to touch him. This purely masculine man seemed to know exactly what she needed, without any question. His tongue teased across her lips as the hand on her hip moved down, curving toward her ass, and gripping the flesh. He held her tightly and without remorse, but she wasn't afraid. Gripping his shirt, she held onto him, refusing to let him go. Her pussy throbbed, and her nipples felt incredibly tight as they pressed against her new shirt.

As she opened her lips, Bain plundered into her mouth, and she touched him with her own tongue, tasting him. He moved them so that he was above her, and she spread her legs so he could rest between them. The hard ridge of his cock pressed against her core, and she cried out, marveling at how big he felt.

Bain broke the kiss, and they were both gasping. "No man has a right to touch you unless it's to give you pleasure. All of those other men were assholes, Scarlett. You deserved so much more." He kissed her lips again, and she whimpered. "Tell me to stop. You have to tell me to stop."

She didn't say a word. Holding the back of his head, she pulled him down, needing more of his kisses. All of her life she had wanted to be the center of someone's world. It was kind of ironic that her life revolved around that of a killer, but still, she was bound to Bain. "I don't want you to stop. I never want you to stop."

He growled, wrapping his arms around her waist, and he lifted them both up. She let out a little squeal and held on for dear life.

"What are you doing?" she asked.

"I'm not going to fuck you on the sofa. You deserve a bed, and that is exactly where I'm going to take you."

She wrapped her legs around his waist. "I don't mind the sofa."

"Not going to happen."

He carried her up to his bedroom. Her weight meant nothing to him as he kicked open his bedroom door and placed her on the bed. She stood up, and he began to work on her clothes. Within seconds she was naked, and Bain picked her up, placing her on the center of the bed.

"I want you to be naked as well."

He was treating her like a delicate princess, and she liked it.

Bain left the bed and removed his clothes, his ink on full display. She mourned the little boy he had once been. Those monsters had molded him into the man he was now, and she just knew there was more to him than he let on. He wasn't as cold as he liked her to think. There was real feeling, real emotion inside him. She was going to be the one to help him to feel. Tonight had proven there was more to him than a simple killer.

His cock was long, hard, and the tip wet with pre-cum. He moved onto the bed, but he didn't go straight between her thighs. He lay down beside her. One of his arms went beneath her head so that she was resting on him. He took hold of one of her hands with his and placed it in the one beneath her head. With her other hand, he trapped it behind his body so that she was defenseless and open.

She was completely at his mercy, and he had a hand free, which landed on her rounded stomach. The heat of that hand rushed through her body, and she pressed her thighs together. Bain could do whatever he wanted to her, and she didn't know what was worse, the fact that she didn't want him to stop, or that she wanted him to use her.

\*\*\*\*

Scarlett's body was a thing of beauty. Bain had fucked many women, young and old. He'd been with women that had enough surgery that their bodies felt like rubber. All of them had wanted something from him, and rarely had it been enjoyable. He had been able to function as if it was just another job. Scarlett, she was natural. She was real, and she was in his bed.

He hated that she tried to suck in her stomach. He loved the rounded stomach as he ran the tips of his fingers over her skin. Her hips were large, and so were her thighs, which were juicy as fuck. He loved her tits as well. Big, with nice pink nipples. He had never been one for loving just one part of a woman, and with Scarlett, each part was his favorite. He loved her tits, her ass, her hips.

What he enjoyed most was her mind. She was hard to pin down. No other woman had made him break the rules.

Sliding his hand up, he cupped her breast. He leaned down and sucked her nipple into his mouth, and she released a beautiful moan. Moving his hand down her body once again, he stroked the tips of his fingers over her breasts, her stomach, and down her thighs. Scarlett went from pressing her thighs together, to spreading them open and thrusting her pelvis up, begging for him to touch her.

She was deprived of touch. He had noticed that, and he'd been trained to know what a woman wanted more than anything. Finally, he cupped her pussy. Her heat and readiness soaked his hand.

"Bain," she said—his name a whimper, a beg. He didn't care. Sliding a single finger through her slit, he found her clit, and circled the bud before moving down to her cunt. With only one digit, he thrust it inside her.

Her pussy tightened around him.

"No man deserved you, baby. None of them knew how to worship your body properly." He eased her off him and moved so that he was between her thighs.

"You don't have to do that," she said.

"Has anyone taken the time to lick this pretty pussy?" he asked.

She shook her head. "No. No. I don't like it. You don't have to do it."

He smiled. "You've not had your pussy licked properly if you don't like it, and believe me, when I finish with you, you're going to love it."

Her hand was covering her mound, and she looked nervous.

Bain slapped her hand, and she let out a little scream. "Trust me. I haven't killed you, have I? You're still living and breathing. Trust me. I'm not going to lie to you."

She glared at him and flopped to the bed.

*Come on, Bain. Make her scream her head off.*

He eased the lips of her pussy open, and she had a pretty one. Flicking the clit, he heard her cry out, gasping. Bain smiled before sucking that bud into his mouth, using his teeth to create a little bite of pain. He teased her entrance, and then slammed his tongue into her cunt. She tasted so damn good, and he loved the sounds she was making. The little squeals were only making him want to hear more of them. While he fucked her cunt, he caressed her clit with his fingers.

Scarlett writhed on the bed. He saw her hands stretch out, fisting the covers.

"Please, don't stop," she said. "It feels so good. Bain!"

Pulling his tongue out of her pussy, he replaced it with his fingers, and then worked on her clit. His cock was swollen with pre-cum soaking the bed where he lay. He wanted so badly to just fuck her hard so that she couldn't walk straight. Instead, he took his time, drawing her close to the edge of orgasm, only he didn't allow her to rush over the peak.

"Do you want me to stop? You don't like a man sucking this pretty pussy."

"No! Don't stop, please. I'm so close."

Running his fingers over her mound, he went back, tasting her once again. This time, he didn't stop. He kept her poised at the edge, refusing to allow her that tumble into bliss. Every second he spent teasing her, he was determined to get her so addicted to him that she couldn't walk away.

*There's nowhere else for her to go.*

He wanted her here of her own free will. For the first time in his life, he wanted this woman. She was the precious gift that he had been given, and he intended to cherish her always. All of his life he had never wanted anything at all. He'd never cared for material shit. He did what he was good at, living life and waiting for death. He wouldn't go willingly, and for the first time in his long, miserable existence, he wanted something more than anything else in the world. He wanted Scarlett to belong to him, to claim her as his own, to possess her, and in return she could have him.

"*Bain! Bain!*" She screamed his name as he thrust her over the edge, and he sucked on her clit, flicking his tongue back and forth as he did. At the same time, his fingers were thrusting inside her tightening pussy. Her back arched, her nipples tightened, and a beautiful flush covered her chest as she shattered apart.

Only when the final aftershocks of her orgasm had ceased did he release her. He moved up her body, licking her excess cream from his face, knowing he would love nothing more than to continue licking her cunt all night long.

Scarlett opened her eyes, and he loved the look of shock in her eyes.

"Do you like having your pussy licked?"

She groaned, covering her face.

He eased her hands away and stared down into her face. Pressing a gentle kiss to her lips, he started to climb off her.

"What are you doing?" she asked.

"I wanted to give you pleasure."

She shook her head and glanced down at his hard cock. "I want you, Bain. This wasn't just about me. I want you. Downstairs, I wanted you inside me." She sat up and moved toward him, her hand circling his cock as she ran it up and down his length. She touched his cheek and kissed him back. "I want you to have the same pleasure that I had."

When she made to wrap her lips around his length, he stopped her and shook his head. "I want to be inside you." He moved her hand away and claimed her lips before she could say anything. Pushing her back to the bed, he was kind of in a surreal moment as she lay against his pillows. Her hair fanned out on his bed. She was like the dream woman he had been waiting a long time for, never expecting to have.

Reaching into his drawer beside his bed, he retrieved a condom and tore open the packet. He'd always kept condoms on hand, just in case. Rolling the latex over his dick, he moved between her thighs. Compared to him she was so much smaller, and he wasn't a small man. He knew how to use his dick, and she was soaking wet. Her orgasm would make it easy for him to take her.

Easing the tip of his cock at her entrance, he began to slide inside her, inch by glorious inch. Her tight pussy sucked him in, and he gripped her hips, watching his cock work inside her body. She was so beautiful to him, and he wanted to keep her, and protect her, and damn it, love her.

He was a cold, hard killer, and he wanted to be the right man for her.

With his grip on her hips, he plunged the last couple of inches, and they both cried out together. Her pussy squeezed his cock.

"You feel amazing," she said. "You're so big."

He released her hips and held her hands, pinning them to the bed. Right now, he was unravelling, and he didn't fucking understand it. Never had he been so consumed, so needy. Scarlett heightened that. She was making him feel, making him want something that he thought had been denied him so long ago.

Slamming his lips down on hers, he ravished her mouth and began to rock inside her. At first he started out slow, allowing her to get accustomed to his size. Then he sped up, thrusting inside her with more force, needing to claim her, to brand her, to mark her as his. That way, every single step that she took, she'd remember who she belonged to.

Breaking from the kiss, he moved toward her pulse, biting down and sucking, and then he moved down to her nipples.

"Please, Bain," she said, moaning his name. Staring into her eyes, he fucked her hard, and then stopped. She wasn't just any woman. This was the woman he wanted, the woman he would protect.

"What is it?" she asked. "What's wrong?"

"Nothing's wrong." In fact, he finally felt like he was waking up, as if he had been doing nothing but sleeping all of his life. "Tell me that you want me."

"I want you, Bain."

Her words were all he needed to hear. He saw that she spoke the truth, even if he was the one to ask her to say those perfect words.

She squeezed his hand and frowned. "What's

happening?" she asked. "Bain, you're crying." Tears fell from his eyes, and he didn't try to hide it. Never from Scarlett. She needed to see the real man he was.

Slowing his thrusts down, Bain did to Scarlett what he had never done to another woman. He made love to her and let her see parts of himself that he had never allowed another to see.

## Chapter Seven

Scarlett twisted amongst the sheets, her body pleasantly sore. She remembered last night and couldn't help but smile. Never in her life had she experienced such equal measures of passion and pleasure. Bain had satisfied her in ways she never knew possible.

By the time she peeked open her eyes, she realized Bain was gone. A moment of panic settled in her gut. She rushed into a sitting position so fast, a wave of dizziness caught her off guard. "Bain!"

His large frame filled the doorway of the bathroom, a white towel around his waist and toothbrush in his mouth. "Yeah, babe?"

Her nerves eased the instant she saw him. The more she fell for Bain, the more she worried he'd be killed because of his line of work. She couldn't lose him.

"Nothing." She tugged the sheets up over her breasts. "Why are you up so early?"

"I have another job. It came in early, and I only have two days to prepare." He disappeared back into the bathroom. She could hear the water flowing into the sink and then the clink of a razor against porcelain.

He was so casual about murder, but she knew he was a killer and still wanted him, so she couldn't really complain. It just felt wrong. Scarlett wondered who the unlucky victim would be this time, and if he deserved what was coming to him or not.

Bain strode into the room, his rock-hard body not easy to ignore. She watched every muscle move and shift as he tugged on a pair of black jeans. He buttoned up and then sat on the edge of the bed with a fresh t-shirt in hand.

"There's something we have to get done today,"

he said. "This friend of yours, the one who knows you went to Semenov's, I need her address."

"What? No!"

He squeezed her thigh. "I didn't say I was going to kill her. But she needs to be dealt with."

"What does that mean, Bain? I told you I'd rather take her place if someone has to pay for something. She doesn't deserve for anything bad to happen to her."

"Look, my boss won't stop until I clean shit up. I still don't know what I'll do about you, but I know for damn sure I can't have that girl running her mouth," he said. Bain slipped the t-shirt over his head, the cotton clinging to his muscles. "We need to find her so you can tell her you're alive and well. Her life's in your hands, so make sure you give her a convincing story. I need her to recant her police report."

"I don't need to give her a story. I want to be here. With you." She touched his neck, tracing her finger along the intricate patterns. "If Lisa believes me, will everything be okay?"

"One thing at a time, sweetheart. You have fifteen minutes. I'll be getting things ready downstairs." He seemed all business again, the previous night's vulnerabilities long forgotten. She didn't want to lose that gentle side of him she was falling in love with.

When he stood, he held the side of her face and kissed her forehead. The single act erased all her misgivings. She exhaled as he left the room.

Scarlett washed up and dressed in the outfit Bain had bought for her last night. She didn't have much else to wear. She wondered if she'd ever be able to go back home to her apartment to get her belongings. Then again, what did the future even hold for her? Did Bain expect her to move in with him? Was she supposed to go back to her old life at some point? She didn't want to pretend none of this happened, to forget Bain and all the drama. He'd come into her life for a reason. She had to believe that.

By the time she went downstairs, he was filling a large black duffel bag with guns of all shapes and sizes. She froze, the reality of her situation hitting her hard.

"Why do we need those just to see Lisa? You said you wouldn't hurt her."

"I'm always prepared. We have a lot of stops to make, and you never know who you'll run into." Bain zipped up the bag and slung it over his shoulder.

She followed him out of the house. "What stops?" she asked.

"First things first. This Lisa chick needs to keep her mouth shut." He dropped the bag into the trunk of his car. "I have some prep to do for my next assignment, and we need to pay your ex a visit."

He moved fast, getting into the driver's seat of the BMW while she stood speechless at the rear of the car. There was no way she wanted to set her eyes on Michael today or ever. But that didn't mean she wanted him dead either, even if he did deserve it.

Scarlett slipped into the passenger seat, the early morning sun reflecting off the face of Bain's watch. It was a high-end Rolex, and it made her think about why he was still living this dangerous lifestyle when he'd already made a fortune. "I don't want to see my ex. Let's just forget about that chapter of my life. It's over."

"It's not over. Not if he's still looking for you."

"The thing with his brother was a fluke. He doesn't know where I am. Hell, I don't even know where I am."

He shifted in his seat, looking directly at her. "You're scared," he said, his voice calm and steady. "Never let your fear do the talking. You have me now."

Scarlett couldn't speak. He was right of course. Deep down, she was still terrified of her ex and the horrible memories she tried to supress. Memories even Bain didn't know about.

"You don't know the half of it. I don't want to see Michael. I can't even stand the sound of his name."

"You and me both." Bain pulled off his property with a spray of gravel and hit the road. The early morning light allowed her to see the gorgeous landscape around Bain's home. Green fields and forests in the distance, not another house in sight. She could never afford to live in the country. Even her basement apartment in the city stretched her budget.

Her thoughts wandered. Scarlett didn't like the idea of Lisa getting involved in this mess. When Bain asked for the address she knew he was testing her loyalty because he was already on his way to Lisa's place. Scarlett hoped she could be convincing enough. How did she expect one of her close friends to believe she'd just decided to quit her job and run off with a stranger with no hint beforehand? Combined with the mass murder scene at Semenov's, it all sounded way too far-fetched.

"This is it," said Bain, after parallel parking like a pro outside Lisa's building.

"You can wait here," said Scarlett. "I'll talk with her and be back soon."

Bain didn't even bother answering her, getting out of the car and waiting for her on the sidewalk with his arms crossed in front of him. She sighed. There was no way he'd let her out of his sight. She was still technically his prisoner until he decided otherwise.

They walked to the front entrance, and she pressed Lisa's buzzer. When she heard her friend's voice, a strange sensation came over her. She'd pushed aside thoughts of her old life, including Lisa, since that night.

Although she hated her job, the constant struggling, and the memories of her horrific love life, Lisa had always been a good friend.

The elevator was broken so they took the stairs up to the third floor. Bain stayed several feet behind her as they walked up the hallway. She knocked on the door, but it opened so fast, her hand was still mid-air.

"Oh my God! I can't believe it's you," Lisa said. "I was going to call the cops today. I thought you were dead." She grabbed Scarlett's arm and pulled her into the apartment. Bain followed, closing the door behind him.

Lisa stared at Bain, a look of apprehension on her face.

"I have to talk to you," Scarlett said. "There's been a huge misunderstanding."

They moved to the far end of the room by the window, but Lisa kept turning her head to glance back at Bain. Once they were out of earshot, Lisa whispered. "Who the hell is that? Is he one of Semenov's men? Are you in trouble?"

"Stop," Scarlett said. "You're being ridiculous."

"Who is he then? Should I call the police?"

"Lisa, relax. He's my … boyfriend. After that scare I got at Semenov's I decided to put everything behind me, to start fresh. You know my career was going nowhere fast at the office."

"Wait, you're starting over. With him?"

"Yes, with him," Scarlett said.

"Look at all those tattoos. He looks like a scary biker. Since when is 'scary biker dude' your type?"

Scarlet was getting worried. If she didn't convince Lisa, she was sure Bain would put a bullet in her head. She gave Lisa a little shake to get her undivided attention. "Lisa, trust me, he's my type. He's literally a sex machine. I'm happy, living my dream, I just wanted to get you up to speed because I know how you worry."

"A sex machine?"

She wasn't joking when she said Bain was a sex machine—he literally was. The man was trained to pleasure women, and she could vouch for his skills after being on the receiving end last night. Just thinking about him made her feel hot and bothered.

"He's good to me, Lisa."

Her friend must have seen it in her eyes, the truth, the love she had for Bain, because Lisa hugged her, pulling her close. "I was so worried. At first when I saw the news, I thought you were dead. Then when no one said anything, I thought you were digging into more research, and then I got scared, and thought something bad had happened. I'm just glad you're okay and that you came to tell me. I was literally about to call the cops."

"Could you do me a favor?" Scarlett asked. "Tell Carter I won't be coming back. I can't face him. It'll be one less researcher he has to let go."

"Sure…"

"Did you tell the police anything?"

"I was going to today. I hadn't heard from you, but you weren't listed as one of the dead. Did you see the carnage on the news? There were almost a dozen bodies."

"I was lucky to have missed it." Scarlett heard Bain clear his throat and knew her time was running out.

Luckily, Lisa seemed too happy that she wasn't six feet under to push her for more information. She hoped it was convincing enough to satisfy Bain.

Once they were back in the car, she sagged against her seat. It was stressful telling her friend half-truths and worrying she wouldn't believe her.

"Was that good enough for you?" she asked.

"We'll see."

They were back on the road again, and she really

just wanted to go home. Where was home? Her apartment was a shitty little prison where she spent her long, lonely nights stressing over every detail of her equally shitty life. Home was wherever Bain was. He made her feel beautiful, special, and safe. Alive rather than existing. What more could she ask for?

"Can we stop at my place to get some clothes?" she asked.

"No way. Your apartment is definitely under surveillance."

She didn't recognize this area of the city, but she was glad they weren't heading to Michael's house. The house they used to share together was the epicenter for her worst nightmares. Bain turned down a side street, then another, before parking the car.

"The suburbs? What now?" she asked, already feeling emotionally exhausted.

"Come on," he said. Bain walked around to the trunk, popped it open, and unzipped that black duffel bag. He tugged on a jacket over his t-shirt, and then concealed a gun in the back of his pants. Every move he made was fast and precise, like he'd done this dance a thousand times.

He shut the trunk and took her hand. The simple act of handholding calmed her nerves and made her connection to Bain grow stronger. She looked at all the different houses, row by row—mowed lawns, flower beds, garden gnomes. Little did the homeowners know a killer was in their midst.

"Where're we going?" she asked.

He stopped and stared at a house across the street. "Time to pay Michael a visit."

\*\*\*\*

Bain had to hold back the beast. All he could think about was breaking that prick's neck. Apparently,

Michael had fucked with Scarlett's head, taught her fear and insecurity, making Bain's job at winning her over harder. It wasn't going to be easy for him to convince Scarlett of her worth, but he'd spend the rest of his life doing it.

That wasn't the only reason he hated the bastard. Michael had bedded Bain's woman and still believed he had a chance with her. Bain needed to stake his claim and set the record straight.

He had a firm grip on Scarlett's hand as they crossed the street. She didn't need to be here for this, but she did need closure, so he'd give it to her.

"Bain, no, I can't…"

"You never have to be scared, baby girl. Not for a fucking second."

"You don't understand." Tears filled her eyes. She clung to him, and his protective instincts fired up inside him. For the first time in his life, he had something of value, something precious. "He didn't just hurt me. There's more."

"What is it?"

"He took something from me—" She couldn't speak any more. Scarlett shook her head, too emotional to continue. Michael really had put her through hell and back.

The wraparound porch was painted white, a wooden rocking chair beside the door. Picture perfect came to mind. Out of all the men he'd killed over the years, the worst of them put up the biggest fronts. They lived in the nicest neighborhoods, had the right friends, and joined the public community events. It was all a façade for the evil lurking beneath. He suspected it was no different with Michael, living in the suburbs, playing house.

"Knock on the door. When he answers, tell him to

you want him to stop looking for you. I'll be close, so don't worry. Can you do that for me?"

She swallowed hard, but nodded. Bain couldn't wait to get this shit over with, because he hated seeing Scarlett so nervous. He had to prove to her that he was capable of handling himself.

He stood farther down the porch while she did as he asked. The door opened, and there was silence. She froze up, staring straight ahead and not able to speak. Bain was about to intervene when Michael spoke.

"I heard you'd moved on, and now … you're here."

"You can't keep looking for me, Michael. Stop trying to get back into my life because it's never going to happen. You know what you did, and it's unforgiveable," Scarlett said.

"You came all the way here to say that? That's doubtful. How'd you find my new address anyway?"

"I have nothing else to say to you. You have no idea how much pain you've caused me. Just keep your distance because I have a court-ordered restraining order."

"You think those mean anything? There not worth the paper they're printed on," he said.

"What's that supposed to mean?"

"Use your imagination, doll." Michael said. "Do you already forget what happens when you piss me off? You think I'm scared of the cops?"

Scarlett started to back away, but the asshole grabbed her arm and forced her into the house. Bain was in the doorway within seconds, kicking the door shut behind him.

"Who the hell is that? Is he the guy you were with?" Michael asked.

"Shut up!" Bain shoved him in the chest, sending

him scrambling backward.

Scarlett grabbed his coat to hold him back. "Bain, no!"

He turned and glared at her. Why was she trying to protect that piece of shit? Did she still love him? Did she have no fucking self-worth?

Bain returned his attention to Michael. He was pathetic, not even worth a bullet. "You like to hurt women?"

"You have no right to be here. This is private property."

He chuckled without humor. "Do you think *I'm* afraid of the cops?"

"This is between me and her," said Michael.

"There is no you and her. Scarlett's mine now. Only mine."

Michael looked toward Scarlett. "Did you actually sleep with this guy?" His face grew redder, his brow lowered. "I knew you were a slut, and this only proves it."

Bain had had enough. He wrapped his hand around the front of his collar and slammed him up against the wall. "Apologize to her," he warned.

It took all his resolve not to empty his clip into this asshole. He'd been raised fighting; it's what he knew and what he loved. Living in regular society had always been a challenge when he was used to acting on impulse, no regard for laws or ethics.

"Get out of my house," Michael said, his voice hoarse with his air supply being limited. When Michael pulled a pocketknife out from his pants, Scarlett screamed.

Bain twisted his arm around his back in one swift move, the knife clanging to the tiled floor. "Fucking apologize, you piece of shit."

"You'll both pay for this," cried Michael.

He leaned down and whispered in the guy's ear. "I fucked that sweet little pussy all night long, tough guy. And I will again tonight. The only cock she'll ever know now is mine. You need to remember that."

Bain stepped back, rolling out his shoulders.

Michael stood up, attempting to straighten his polo shirt. "Keep her. She's damaged goods now. I don't know what I was thinking hooking up with that. I have standards."

Bain groaned, his temper flaring. No one insulted Scarlett. This was supposed to be enlightening for her, not make her feel like trash. When he heard her sobbing, he lost it, punching her ex in the mouth.

"You *wish* you had a woman like her." Another punch to ensure he kept his fat mouth shut. "But you fucked up, and now she's mine."

When he heard several car doors slam shut, he peered out the window.

*Fuck me!*

Boss and three of his men were coming up the walkway. Bain had to protect Scarlett. If he had to he'd end the four of them, but it would guarantee a life of running, constantly looking over his shoulder.

Killian shoved open the door. The Irish prick was one of Boss's newest acquisitions. He was cutthroat and heartless, not the type of man Bain wanted coming after Scarlett. His sadistic smile faded when he saw Scarlett standing against the wall in the foyer. It was rumored Killian never accepted contracts on women.

"Well, well, well. Look at this," said Boss as he strolled in with two other hitmen. "I warned you to clean up your shit, Bain. Did I not warn you?"

"I have everything under control." Now that the Lisa knew Scarlett was alive and well, there weren't any loose ends. The original witness wasn't a problem because she belonged to Bain now.

"Obviously not if I've wasted my morning doing clean up when I had plans to hit the gym. That doesn't put me in a good mood," said Boss.

One of the hitmen took a step toward Scarlett, and Bain instinctively drew the gun from his back, aiming it at the man's face. "Don't even fucking breathe on her," he warned.

"Interesting," said Boss. "I remember Viper telling me they'd fucked you up beyond the point of no return when you were a kid. Now, look at this. Ready to kill poor Carlos for a piece of pussy." He shrugged and strolled around the room, a gun swinging in his hand.

"What's going on?" asked Michael.

All attention diverted to him after he spoke. "And who the hell is this little fuck? I don't have any guy on my loose-end list, just the two women. Well, one woman," said Boss, scratching his forehead with the muzzle of his gun. "Are you trying to make this more difficult for me on purpose, Bain?"

"Leave Lisa alone!" Scarlett said. She was terrified, but brave when it came to helping others. He liked that about her.

"Was that her name? I'd forgotten already," said Boss. "Well, I've cleaned up that epic disaster since you couldn't, and now we're here."

"You killed her?" Scarlett asked. She started crying uncontrollably, but Bain couldn't take his eyes off Boss or his men just yet. Dogs barked in the distance, the hum of a lawnmower drowning out Scarlet's sobs. It was a regular morning for the neighborhood.

Boss ignored her. "Care to finish this up, Bain? Despite your unrefined methods, I can still see your value. I won't be cutting you loose just yet."

Bain moved his outstretched arm, shifting to point the handgun at Michael. It wasn't a hard decision considering he'd wanted that fucker dead the moment Bain knew of his existence. As long as he was alive, that deep-seated fear would live on in Scarlett. Those memories and secrets needed to be terminated permanently. When he'd escaped his captors as a teen, murdering them all didn't erase the nightmares, but it helped.

Bain pulled the trigger.

## Chapter Eight

Michael fell in a heap with blood spattering the wall. Scarlett didn't feel anything for the evil bastard now that he was dead. He had taken so much from her and made her feel more pain than anyone ever had. Michael was part of the reason why she would have gladly found peace in her own death.

Lisa was her problem. Her best friend was dead. No, she couldn't be dead. Scarlett wouldn't believe it. Lisa was a sweet woman. She stared at the man who seemed to be the leader, the one doing most of the talking and not a lot of listening.

"Now, why do you have a problem with doing that to this one right here?" The man yelled as he pointed from Michael's body to her.

"Boss, I told you to back out of it, and I mean it." Bain grabbed her hand, and he had a gun raised at the men. She held onto Bain, and wondered, not for the first time, why she felt safe with him. He might be a murderer, but her ex had been so much worse to her.

*Michael hurt me so badly that he killed my baby. He was a monster.*

She held in her sob, refusing to let her painful memories distract Bain. He didn't know. No one knew how Michael had thrown her downstairs, and repeatedly kicked her in the stomach and back until she miscarried on the floor. He wouldn't take her to the hospital for the longest time, and when he did Scarlett was forced to lie about the violence. She had to see the painful evidence of what she had lost.

Had it made her a little mad in the head? She didn't know.

Boss sighed, and then he began to pace. He took

four steps one way and four steps the other. For someone who paced he was rather precise in how he dealt with his steps. She felt crazy for being hypnotized by the way someone walked.

"You have one job to do and that's to do exactly what I say."

"Fuck you, Boss. I did what you wanted."

"No. You left mess following in your wake. For someone who's supposed to know what they're doing, you're sloppy. You're not professional. You're nothing like fucking Viper was."

"Then hire him back. Remember, you came to me. You wanted me, not the other way around. I do my work, and I get the job done."

"Then kill her!" Boss yelled. "Kill her. Prove to me right now that you can follow orders. Grab her damn neck and put a bullet inside her. She's a problem, Bain. Do what you know you can do. What's easy for you to do."

Bain's hand tightened around hers. It wasn't painful yet, but it was getting close. "I kill the people you need me to, but I'm not going to do this."

Why did Bain sound so calm?

Boss exhaled, an exasperated sound. "You know, I had my doubts about you, and every step of the way you're proving I was right to doubt myself." He snapped his fingers, and the men with him held their guns up.

She gasped as Bain let her go and held his own gun steady. He didn't train it on anyone else but Boss. "You really want to do this?" Bain asked.

"I clean up my mess."

"There's no problem here," Bain said. "But I'll put a bullet in your fucking skull if you don't back up, and I mean that."

"You don't have the fucking—" Boss didn't get to

finish as Bain shot him in the shoulder. Boss groaned and cursed. His jaw clenched as he pressed a hand to his shoulder. The three men with him didn't do anything. They continued to hold their guns on them, nothing happening.

Bain had just shot their boss, so why weren't they shooting? She expected a replay of the gunfight at Semenov's. Her heart raced, and her entire body trembled. Bain had moved her so that she was shielded by his body. She held onto his waist, hoping that she gave him strength even as hers was fading fast.

"You shot me?"

"You were going to tell me I didn't have the fucking balls. I do, Boss. I don't give a fuck if you live or die. All of my life I've never had anything to myself. I've given you everything. I've given everyone who ever wanted anything, everything. There's nothing left to give. You're not having her. I'm not giving her up. Not for you. Not for Killer of Kings. For no one."

The emotion in his voice shocked her. He was on the brink. Couldn't anyone else sense that? They all stood facing off against one another, and Bain was fighting for her. No one had ever fought for her. No one cared enough about her. She was always a means to an end. Something to be disposed of or replaced.

The tension was thick. Silence fell in the house, and she was sure that she could hear a pin drop. Time seemed to stand still they waited for one of them to make the first move.

There was the sound of another car door closing, and Boss was the first one to mutter. "Is this fucker popular?"

One of the men left and looked through the curtains. "Viper is here."

"You've got to be fucking kidding me," Boss

said, moving toward the door. "Is this a family fucking reunion?"

The door opened, and another deadly looking guy entered the house, a gnarly scar down one half of his face. "I see I've come in time."

"Viper, what the fuck are you doing here?" Bain asked.

"I may be out of the business, but a contracted killer never really steps away. I've got a woman to protect, and a family business to keep thriving." Viper frowned and pointed to Michael. "You know this guy?"

"No. I don't know him, but he hurt my woman, and so he couldn't live another day. He hurt her, and I think he did a whole lot of other shit I don't even know about."

"So he was a piece of scum," Viper said. He pushed his hands into his pockets.

All of this was surreal to her as she was in Michael's home with a bunch of killers, hitmen. Deadly weapons for hire for a really high price.

*Crap.*

The man she hated more than anything was now dead, and people had seen her enter the neighborhood. Would they think she killed him? Wow, she was starting to feel really sick right now, and everything that was happening around her scared her.

*Breathe, Scarlett, breathe.*

"I want to know why you're here, Viper," Boss said.

"You came for a party and seeing as I consider Bain an actual brother—"

"You do?" Bain asked. She heard the confusion in his voice now.

"We took an oath, Bain. You and me, we shared blood, and we bound ourselves together. I won't kill you.

I've told you that many times, and I mean it."

Did he mean the blood oath? Scarlett stared down at her hand and wondered just how many people Bain had shared blood with. Before doubts flooded her mind, she remembered he had said that he'd only ever shared blood once before. That other person had to be Viper, which meant he was with him when they were kids.

She really needed to lie down. She was starting to feel a little lightheaded with the information overload that was happening. Not to mention being in Michael's house, his dead body only feet away. It had taken her a long time to finally gain the self-respect to leave his horrible ass.

"So why the fuck are you here?" Bain asked. "You're out of the business. You're not supposed to be part of this."

She felt his back vibrating, and she tried to offer him some comfort with her touch.

"I needed to make sure you were doing the right thing. You're not used to working for someone else. It's a lot different than going solo." Viper looked at her. "Is she worth all of this?"

"You don't get to fucking look at her. I cleaned up my fucking mess, and you, you did what you fucking wanted. Or don't you remember?"

"Killer of Kings has a reputation to uphold, Bain. You've got to do things by a certain code. She's a loose end," said Viper.

"She's mine!" Bain growled. Scarlet held him tightly from behind. She didn't care if it looked stupid, but she needed him to know she was here if he needed her. Silence once again fell between them. "You're not taking her away from me. I'm going to go and put her in the car, and you're going to stay here. I'll be right back."

"Go with him," Boss said, pointing to one of the scary looking guys.

They put their guns away, and Bain was suddenly leading her out of the house. The moment they passed Boss, Bain pulled her around to the front so that she was completely covered at all times.

"Bain, what's going on?" she asked.

"I'm going to have a nice long chat with these assholes, and then we're going to go back home where I'm going to spend the rest of our day fucking." They got to his car, and he leaned forward, opening the door. "I want you to drive fast and far away from here."

"No."

"You've got nothing to be afraid of. I'll find you when I'm done."

"I'm not running. I'm not going to go somewhere and risk never seeing you again. If you die today, and you don't come out of that house, then I don't go either, and I'm dead."

"Everyone who could hurt you is gone," said Bain. "I want you to be happy."

He was so sweet. It was the strangest thought and feeling in the world to have about a killer. He wasn't evil to her. Bain was many things, but she was falling in love with him. He was hard and yet not. He inspired so many emotions inside her, and she couldn't walk away, or leave him.

"I'm going to handle this." He handed her a gun. "For me, if I don't come out of that house first, I want you to live. You have to do that for me. You have to live."

Tears filled her eyes, falling down her cheeks. "No. I don't want to live without you. Don't make me do this."

He cupped her cheeks and once again pulled her in for a kiss. "Do as I say."

"He killed Lisa," she whispered.

"I'm going to deal with this, baby. Trust me, okay."

With that, he turned and ordered the other man to follow him. She climbed into the car and watched as he entered the house. Staring down at the gun in her hand, it would be so easy to end her miserable life, but what if Bain came out of that house? Today had gone from being one of the best days of her life to suddenly one of the worst. There was no way she could live without Bain, not now, not after falling in love. She would rather die than be without him.

Staring at the gun, she made her decision. If Bain didn't walk out that door, she was going to end her own life.

****

Bain was pissed off and frustrated. This hadn't gone the way he wanted it to go. He'd wanted Scarlett to find some kind of solace or closure. At the very least he wanted her to face her demons like he had done all of those years ago. Instead of helping the situation, all he did was make it worse, and now he felt even shittier about it.

Staring at Viper as he entered Michael's home, he saw his somewhat-friend was worried. Bain never really knew where to place Viper in his life. When they were younger Viper had given him hope when he'd been short on faith. After breaking out, they had been partners, joined together in riding the world. Over the years they'd found their way back to each other at random points. The last time, Viper had found the love of his life and left Killer of Kings. Bain had been his replacement.

Staring at Boss, he wanted to kill the man but knew he couldn't. Something in his gut told him that whoever killed Boss would end up with a massive hit on their head. It would only be a matter of time before they were dead. "You want to tell me why the fuck you're tailing me?" Bain asked.

"I already told you. I'm cleaning up after your mess, and, Bain, you're making a lot of fucking mess," Boss said. The owner of Killer of Kings looked down over Michael. "He's not a fucking kill. Why is he dead? Why isn't that bitch outside dead? Why wasn't that other woman dead? I thought you were going to handle it. You haven't done one single thing that I asked you to do. Killer of Kings is a reliable service. We have guarantees in place, which is why people pay a fucking fortune for the right to use us, and not some back-alley piece of shit."

Bain glared at the other man. "Everything was handled. I kill who needs to be killed. That is all I do. This was something I was dealing with for Scarlett. She's not your problem. She's mine."

"She's a loose end. One you need to learn to cut the fuck off."

Bain didn't think about what he did next, he simply reacted. Grabbing Boss around the neck, he had him pressed against the nearest wall with a gun at his temple. "You do not get to tell me what I fucking do. Do you understand me? You will leave Scarlett out of this. She was not your concern. She will never be your concern."

"You're part of Killer of Kings, asshole. Everything you do is my concern. Whether you breathe, piss, fuck, take a shit, it's all relevant to me. You gave everything up to be on my books, and that is how it'll fucking stay." Boss had no fear. He was calm, his confidence off the fucking charts. Bain supposed he had the muscle and skill to back it up, but right now he didn't care.

"Bain, let him go," Viper said.

"No. I should fucking kill him right now. End

this."

"You kill him, it will only start a war you can never win. Boss is number one. Always has been, always will be."

"You can't tell me that you've not thought about ending him. Taking him out," Bain said.

"More times than I could count, but it's not worth it. He's not worth this."

"Now you two are just breaking my fucking heart," Boss said.

Bain stared at the devil himself. Boss could joke and make everyone think he was a sane best friend. He saw the truth. Boss was a monster. It was how he'd been able to stay on top for so long. Boss did the job no one else could.

Removing his weapon, Bain backed up, but he didn't go far. "You *will* leave Scarlett alone."

"Why is she so important to you?" Boss asked.

"Because she's my woman. She belongs to me."

"There are a million women out there, all with the same kind of pussy. Fuck them. Don't fuck the woman who watched you murder those men."

"She's mine!" Bain yelled the word, and Viper stepped between them.

"Get them out of here," Viper said.

Boss ordered the three men out, and Bain had no choice but to stop them. "Go out the back door. I told my woman to take off if she sees anyone else but me leave the house."

"For fuck's sake. Pussy whipped the lot of you. Go out the damn back," Boss said.

Within seconds they were alone.

"What's going on here?" Boss asked. "You're giving me a headache."

"I want Scarlett. I'm not negotiating that."

"Are you telling me you're coming out of the life?"

"No. I can't stop what I do," said Bain. "I need to kill."

"And you're not going to give her up?" Boss asked.

"I can't."

"She's just a piece of pussy."

"To everyone else but not to me," Bain said. "I need her. She's mine, and you can't take her away from me."

"This is why I wanted the others gone," Viper said. "When we were kids, you know what we went through. Don't pretend you didn't. You fucking knew everything. We had nothing. Every time we tried to find some shred of love or anything, they tore it from us and made us either destroy it, or watch it die. We have never had anything in our lives to call our own. The homes. The material shit. They mean nothing. They are nothing to us. He wants Scarlett. Let him have her. You have nothing to lose."

Bain kept his mouth shut. He wasn't interested in playing nice right now. Every time Boss spoke, he wanted to kill him.

The only thing that kept him at bay was the woman outside waiting for him, and the future he planned for the two of them. A real family.

Boss groaned. "Fine. You know what, have the woman, but if this little obsession fades away, you will deal with her, understood?"

"Yes," said Bain.

"You will also stay on at Killer of Kings. I'm not going to have you quit on me. However, you have the rest of the month off until this honeymoon period is over."

"You're not going to take a hit out on me?" Bain

asked.

"No. I'm not. I see your value yet. But you'll do as I say, and there'll be a price for this little gift you gave me." He touched the bleeding wound on his shoulder.

"What about Lisa? Scarlett talked to her, and she handled everything. All that woman knew was that Scarlett had a boyfriend and had been with me for the past week."

"She's dead, Bain. Obviously. I told you I tied up loose ends, and she was one of them."

"She didn't have to die."

Boss chuckled. "This is why none of you will ever best me. You can never do the job that needs to be done. She was innocent until she had the potential to incriminate us. Now, she's dead. Poor thing killed herself in the bathtub." He stepped up close. "Next time I tell you to clean up your shit, you will do it, as otherwise, I'll make sure *you're* the loose end. Get the fuck out, and I'll clean up this mess."

Bain wanted to pound the fucker's face. Instead, he walked out with Viper close behind him. He looked toward the car and saw Scarlett's relief. He smiled and gave her a wave.

"You love her?" Viper asked.

"Yes."

"Is she worth having Boss pissed off with you?"

"Was Pepper worth it?" Bain asked, not looking away from Scarlett. She had rested her head back and looked like she was smiling. Part of him had expected her to be long gone by now. She hadn't left him, and that just made him happy.

"You know she was. I was on my way to kill her. Things changed," Viper said.

"Scarlett gives me peace, and when I'm with her, the past ceases to exist for me. I can't let her go, and I won't." Finally, he turned to look at his friend. "You didn't have to come today. I was fine."

Viper shrugged. "I have my ways of keeping an eye on you. Boss can be a big asshole, and I knew you didn't deserve to die."

"You don't have to keep an eye on me. I can take care of myself, and I've been doing it for a long time."

"I guess it's hard to just let you go after all this time," Viper said.

They shared a bond. It was a strange one and not one he liked thinking about all that much. "I promised her I would keep her safe. We shared blood, which I think grossed her out a little." He smiled.

"That's a big step with you."

"She's going to be upset though," said Bain.

"Why?"

"Her friend Lisa's dead, and I promised her I wouldn't lay a hand on her."

"You didn't. Boss did. A little piece of advice, when he says he's going to do something, he will. No questions asked. He owes you for shooting him, so watch your back," he said. "I've got to be heading home. Pepper didn't want me to come, but I couldn't let you face this alone."

"Bye, Viper." Bain made his way toward the car and climbed behind the wheel. He didn't linger and pulled away from the curb, heading home.

They were alive, safe, and together.

"I didn't anticipate what went down in there," said Bain.

"Which part?"

"All of it. I expected Michael to see your strength, your beauty. He was an asshole. You never have to worry about him again."

"And Lisa?"

He sighed. His heart ached for his woman's pain. This was the last thing he wanted her to go through. Her tears meant more to him than anything else. The moment she cried, it was like he'd failed at keeping her happy. "I'm sorry."

"That man is a monster. Why didn't you just kill him?" she asked.

He chuckled. "I was going to, but Boss is the top boss because he makes sure everyone else is in hell. I pull that trigger, and Boss dies at my hand, and it will be a matter of days if not hours before I join him. I'd be hunted to the ends of the earth."

"You're kidding, right? There's no way that would happen. He'd be dead."

Bain took her hand, pressing a kiss to her knuckles. "Killer of Kings would live on. That's why he's the strongest and most powerful. There is no limit to what Boss will do."

It was why he needed to keep Scarlett far away from Boss, just in case the fucker had a change of heart.

## Chapter Nine

When Scarlett saw Bain's house come into view, she felt an instant sense of ease. If only the whole world could disappear, leaving just the two of them in this little piece of paradise. Bain might be used to his unorthodox lifestyle, but she was still in shock. How could she ever feel comfortable with constant death and danger?

They pulled onto the long gravel drive to the old farmhouse. It was a simple brick two-storey with unkempt lawn, but it was homey and inviting. When he turned off the ignition, silence settled in. She realized neither of them had spoken the entire drive home. Her thoughts were scattered in so many directions.

"What will happen to Michael?" she asked.

"Boss will handle everything. It's what he does."

She nodded. It was hard to get the vision of her ex's dead body out of her mind, even though she felt a newfound peace knowing he was gone. The only way for her to stay sane was to convince herself Michael deserved his fate—he'd killed the innocent baby growing inside her.

"You shot your boss. Why didn't he shoot back? There were four of them."

"I have to remind myself that fucker is even human. Maybe he doesn't feel pain," said Bain, his hands squeezing the steering wheel. "I don't like how he let me off so easy."

"He must see your value."

Bain took a deep breath and got out of the car. She chased after him as he entered the house.

"Who were all those men? Did you know them?" she asked. Scarlett had a feeling Bain didn't want to talk about this, but she couldn't just pretend nothing happened. It helped her to talk things out. She had so many questions.

"Viper was the one I told you about, the one I grew up with. He's the only person I'd have to think twice about before killing. He wanted to make sure I didn't do anything stupid because he was the one to put a good word in for me at Killer of Kings. Maybe it wasn't such a bad thing that he showed up. When it comes to you, I seem to jump the gun."

"He loves you. I could see it in his eyes."

"I wouldn't go that far," he said. "But out of the five of them, he'd be the least likely to pull the trigger."

"What about the others?"

"I know Boss and his new right-hand man, Killian. I haven't seen the other two before, but I've only met a fraction of the people working for Killer of Kings."

He braced both hands on the kitchen counter, his back to her. She put one hand over his. "Will everything be okay?" she asked.

His mood seemed to shift, as if he realized how distant he'd become. Bain smiled as he turned around. "I'm sorry, baby." He held her head against his chest, his other arm keeping her close. "This must be scary for you. I keep forgetting you're not used to any of this shit."

"I just want to be happy. I'm tired of getting the short stick in life."

Bain tilted her chin up. "Things will be different now. You're mine, and everyone knows it. Boss gave me the rest of the month off, so I'm all yours."

"Really?"

"Do whatever you want to me." He winked.

God, he had such a ruggedly handsome face. She could stare at him all day. And his body … just envisioning his ripped body made her think very X-rated thoughts.

"You said we'd spend the rest of the day … you know."

He scooped her up into his arms without warning. She wasn't light, but he carried her upstairs as if she weighed a hundred pounds. Bain brought her to a bathroom in the upstairs hallway. It had been renovated with a walk-in shower. He set her down and started the water.

"After every job, I like to come in here and take a long shower. It's cleansing, you just imagine the water washing away the shit in your head." He pulled her shirt up and off, her hair fanning down on her back. "You do the same thing, okay, Scarlett? Forget what you saw today. Let it all wash away."

"It's okay, Bain. You don't have to protect me." She slipped out of her capris until she was standing in her bra and panties. "And I don't blame you for anything. I'm glad you did what you did."

He cupped her cheeks and gave her one soft kiss. "I can't stand the thought of you being a part of my world. You're too good for this, and I don't want to poison you."

"I'm more broken than you think," she said. "Maybe two halves can make a whole?"

She saw the emotion in his eyes because it reflected her own. He was nothing like the man she'd first seen at Semenov's.

Bain groaned as he tugged off his shirt. "Tonight, we're going to forget about everything. There's nothing else. It's just you and me."

"Okay," she whispered.

Once they were both undressed, Bain slid open the large glass door so they could step inside. The warm water flowed down from the rainfall shower heads. He was right. There was something healing about the water tracing down her hair and face, the old being washed away, replaced with hope and new beginnings.

Bain's large frame towered over her. He braced one hand on the shower wall, the other settling on the small of her back. He brought her close until there was only a breath between them. "You're beautiful, Scarlett. More than I deserve."

"Don't say that," she said. "You're a good man."

He chuckled. "You won't think so after tonight." Bain kissed her on the mouth, the water rushing down around them. Her need that had been put on the back burner returned with a vengeance. His hard, tattooed body kept coming closer until she was pressed to the tiled wall. She could feel his desire, his masculine energy surrounding her. Scarlett rested a hand on each of Bain's biceps, savoring the feel of his muscles flexing. She closed her eyes as he kissed her neck, his tongue tracing patterns along her erogenous zones.

"That feels so good," she said.

"I can't get enough of you." He returned to her lips, devouring, tasting, claiming. The roughness of his stubble scratched her cheeks, but she didn't care. His strength aroused her. He could snap her in two or put a bullet in her head, but Bain loved her, wanted her. It was addicting to tame such a beast.

They managed to dry off a bit and make their way to his bedroom. Unlike the night before, the sun hadn't set so there would be no hiding their nudity. Normally she'd be a bit uncomfortable, but she'd passed that point of no return in the shower. All she wanted was to feel Bain filling her, taking her again and again. She'd had other men, and it only confirmed that he was beyond average, any woman's fantasy, and all hers.

She wanted to give him something more, to wrap her lips around his big dick. They both needed an escape, to give up complete control in exchange for new, wicked pleasures. Scarlett bent over, kissing her way down his hard abs on her way to his erect cock. Her mouth salivated with her desire to taste him, to feel him between her tongue and pallet. She wrapped her hand around the base and licked the smooth tip.

"No, Scarlett, don't." He pulled away, sitting on the bed. "Let me make love to you."

Was she doing it wrong? He had such a beautiful cock, perfect actually, like the rest of him. Didn't men like their woman to go down on them? She desperately wanted to pleasure him at the same time as she craved to explore his body.

When she looked at him, she realized his chest was rising and falling rapidly, as if he'd just been frightened or run a few laps. "Are you okay? What's wrong with you?"

He shook his head. "Nothing. Come here, baby. Let me make you feel good."

Something didn't feel right. She didn't want to just take and never give back. It wasn't fair. Scarlett stood between his parted legs, and he cupped her ass in his palms, taking her areola into his mouth. She moaned, her pussy pulsing in response. Bain was so damn good at what he did. He almost made her forget everything.

"No." She moved away. "Why won't you let me go down on you?"

"You don't want to do that," he said.

"Really? You're wrong, Bain. I want to. Did I do it wrong? You can teach me the way you like it."

He tried to reach for her, but she wouldn't let him.

"Scarlett, it's just something I can't handle. It makes me fucking anxious. Even sex, it took me a long time before I could get any pleasure from it. With you, things are different. But—"

"How is it different from sex?"

Bain wouldn't look her in the eyes. He patted his lap, and she willingly sat down, wrapping an arm around him. She couldn't stop kissing and touching him.

"When I was younger, I was forced to let women use me. My captors would hurt me if I did anything wrong, and the punishment didn't stop until I was perfect. They did a lot of wicked shit to me, Scarlett. I didn't enjoy what I did, I hated it. Ever since that fucking chapter of my life closed, there are certain things that I can't really get over. You know what I mean?"

He'd been forced, so it was no different than rape. No wonder he had issues with his sexuality. Her love for him grew, as did her need to heal him.

"I'm different, Bain. I'd never hurt you."

He kissed her shoulder, and she held his head against her chest. Scarlett could only imagine the horrors he'd been through. She couldn't stand to see him so broken, unable to trust or put the pieces of himself back together. It wasn't much different than her take on life. They were so different, but also so much alike.

"It's not so simple," he said. "Not when the past fucks with your head."

If she wanted him to trust her, she had to do the same. "Remember I told you about Michael and the secrets I kept? Well, I was going to have a baby." Tears filled her eyes before she could finish. The pain was still fresh, as if it happened yesterday, not over a year ago. "I lost it before it was born. Because of Michael's abuse."

She felt Bain's hold on her grow tighter. "That's not a secret, Scarlett. It wasn't your fault."

"I should have left him," she cried, the tears flowing freely. She shook her head, still so angry with herself. "If I'd had a backbone I would have left, and I'd be a mother today. But I'm not. I'm nothing. I have nothing. And I can never forgive myself." She felt so stupid being naked and crying. She was a hot mess.

"I know what being abused can do to a person. You become a shadow of yourself, unable to distinguish between reality and the fucked-up shit they want you to believe. It's not your fault, sweetheart." He'd raised his voice to express his point, and it surprised her that this man could care so much about her suffering when he originally planned on killing her. She hadn't told anyone her shameful secret and wouldn't have believed anyone's sympathy regardless. Bain was different. She knew only Bain could understand how her head had been so messed up when she'd been with Michael. He'd devastated her confidence until she was a shell of a woman, and the abuse stole all her strength.

"How do you go on?"

He smirked and looked up at her. "You do like me. You survive, you exist. I killed to quiet the demons inside me. It wasn't until you came into my life that I realized there could be more."

She smiled, more tears flowing, but they weren't from self-pity. "I want to be happy with you," she said.

\*\*\*\*

Bain knew all about Scarlett's miscarriage from the hospital records, but refused to bring it up. It was her choice whether she shared that with him or not. The fact she'd opened up to him, releasing all that pent-up pain and tension, made him feel closer to her.

"I need you," he said.

The vulnerable moment shifted to more passion than he'd ever known. He wanted to own Scarlett, to claim her, to keep her for himself. The thought of any man coming between them seriously pissed him off.

They dropped down on the bed, intertwined, not able to get enough of each other. His cock was heavy and stiff. He couldn't wait to slide deep inside Scarlett's pretty little cunt, marking her as his again and again. With her, sex was exactly how it should be, and the only time he was grateful for his training in the bedroom.

"Oh God, Bain. I want you."

He kissed his way down her neck, flipping her to her back so he could play with her big tits. Bain rubbed his face in her cleavage, then took her nipple in his mouth, teasing her until she arched her back.

When her little hand wrapped about his cock, his eyes lolled back in his head. "I want to taste you, Bain. Please…"

Those bitches had ruined him for sex, hurting him in inhumane ways. His captors were hell-bent on creating a killing machine made for fucking. He knew he could trust Scarlett, she was sweet and caring, but he couldn't get over his own damn insecurities. Bain hated having a weakness, and he didn't want it to rule his life forever.

"You don't have to do that," he said.

"I want to. I love you."

Those words felt unreal, and his instincts expected deception. He usually killed when he felt pushed against the wall, but for Scarlett he seemed ready to take on the world.

She crawled along his body, her nails gently dragging down his torso. When she reached his cock, Bain cringed, but he forced himself to stop living in the past. He ran his hand through her silky hair, focusing on how much he wanted this one woman.

Her mouth was warm and wet as it covered his swollen head. She moved slowly, cautiously, her free hand wrapped firmly around the root of his dick. Bain closed his eyes, savoring the feel of her lips taking him deeper, her tongue tracing the sensitive vein with each upstroke. Scarlett wouldn't hurt him, and this was his choice. With each passing minute, he began to relax and truly enjoy the gift she gave him.

He watched her head bobbing up and down over his cock, bringing him closer to coming down her throat. But he wanted to be inside her, fucking her until she screamed his name.

"That's enough, baby. Let me have some fun with you," he said. Bain sat up, pulling Scarlett over his lap so she straddled him. "Put it in. Put my cock inside that hot little pussy."

She struggled, her chest heaving as she forced his erection inside her. As soon as he entered her, she sat down hard, moaning and grabbing his shoulders for support. She was so tight, so perfect.

"Oh yeah, that's a good girl." He watched her tits bounce as she began to fuck him, rising up and slamming down, over and over. The sounds she made spurred him on, his balls pulling up tight. "Make me come. I want to feel you milking my cock."

After nearly bringing him to the edge, she came down heavily, her breathing erratic. "I can't. I'm too tired," she said.

He smiled, knowing he was capable of fucking her all night long, every night. Bain grabbed her hips, twisting them around until he dominated, his cock still deep inside her. He kissed her lips, licking and nipping as he brushed the moistened hairs from her face. "You're mine, Scarlett. I'll do anything for you, fuck you any time you ask, kill anyone who hurts you."

"Yes," she murmured, writhing beneath him. "Make me yours."

Her confirmation satisfied the beast within him. He began to fuck her, all his energy expelled as he pistoned his hips like a machine, making sure to satisfy his woman completely.

When her pussy began to spasm around him, he knew she was moments away. "Come for me. Let it all go, baby."

As soon as she cried out, her nails digging into his back, he relaxed enough to let go, spilling his seed inside her. It was a raw moment. This was the first day he hadn't lied to himself, hadn't convinced himself he was a worthless bastard not deserving of love.

They were both spent, lying next to each other as they caught their breath. When he heard someone knocking on his front door, the hollow sound echoed through the old house, he bolted out of the bed. "Stay here," he said, his breathing still rapid.

"Who is it?"

"I don't know. Nobody comes here." He tugged on a pair of sweatpants and grabbed a Glock from the bedside table. "Don't leave this room."

Bain rushed down the stairs. Whoever was at his door was lucky they hadn't interrupted him a few minutes earlier or he'd really be pissed off. His barriers came down for Scarlett only, and he still didn't give a shit about anyone else.

He yanked open the door, ready for anything, even Boss, but it was Killian. Bain looked around, and saw no one else with him and only one vehicle parked in his driveway.

"Why the fuck are you here? And how'd you get my address?"

Had Boss sent him to clean up loose ends, to kill him dead? He could try.

"Consider it a courtesy call. A friendly warning."

This fucker was Boss's personal bodyguard, so there was no way Bain trusted a word he said. Everyone who worked for Killer of Kings was loyal to the cause, including Viper.

"I'm listening."

"I don't like to see innocent women getting messed up in our shit, but Boss, he doesn't have the same idea." Killian ran a hand through his dark blond hair. The sides were shaved, the top long and pushed back. The scar through his upper lip always made him look like he was snarling. A damn pretty boy straight up from hell.

"If you have something to fucking say, say it."

Killian smirked. "Did you think you'd get away with shooting Boss?"

"It was a clean shot to the shoulder. He didn't look too upset," said Bain.

"You fucking shot him, Bain. That doesn't go unpunished. He plans to get his revenge on the girl."

Bain frowned. That piece of shit had said he wouldn't kill Scarlett, even gave him the rest of the month off. He knew joining Killer of Kings was a mistake. He'd never had these problems working solo contracts. "He lied to me then."

"He's not going to kill her. You know the game. An eye for an eye."

"I won't let him shoot her, either. For fuck's sake, I won't let him near her." Bain had watched Boss shoot Viper's woman without a hint of emotion in his cold, dead eyes. There was no way he could allow that to happen to Scarlett.

Killian pulled out a pack of smokes, hitting the pack until one came out. He lit up and took a long drag. "Can't say I'm crazy about it. That's why I'm here, eh?"

He'd heard rumors about Boss's Irish hitman, the one who had a soft spot for women. Until right now, he'd thought he was a waste of breath.

"You know, this house call isn't much help. Boss can find us anywhere we go. If he's set on hurting Scarlett, he won't stop until he gets his way."

"A man can be convinced of anything. Look at you—"

"What about me?" Bain asked.

"Boss has had a hard-on to sign you up for years, said you were the devil himself. But look at you now, falling for a woman you've known for a few days." Killian blew out a cloud of smoke, a wicked smile on his fucked up lips.

"Thanks for the heads-up, but you can fuck off now. If Boss gives the order, tell him I'll kill him before I let him near my woman."

Killian shrugged. "Have a nice night, bud." He stomped out his cigarette and got into his car, driving away without another word. Bain watched the billow of dust until the car disappeared from distance down the country road. He really needed to invest in a front gate.

Bain spat before closing the door. It figured that as soon as he found something worth living for, fate was ready to fuck with him again. Boss and Killian, and the whole damn world, might think he'd gone soft because of Scarlett. They were wrong.

## Chapter Ten

*Four days later*

Scarlett stretched her arms above her head and stared up at the ceiling fan. Last night had been another dream come true with Bain completely at her mercy. She loved how he caved, how he loved having her mouth on him. There was no way she could even begin to imagine how he must have felt as a child being forced to commit those kinds of acts. She didn't want to think about it.

Children were supposed to be protected, enjoyed, loved, not used as toys in a game. That was what he'd been forced to endure. They had all been toys, playing some disgusting game. Sitting up in bed, she reached out and already knew she would find Bain's space empty. He rarely slept late, nor did he go to sleep early either. She would promise herself each night that she would be the last to fall asleep, and each night, she'd be the first to fall. It didn't help that he would spend what felt like hours stroking her hair.

Each touch promised her safety and love. She had never known love, not really.

Pushing the blankets off, she climbed out of bed, grabbed a shirt, and went in search of him. Every morning she would find him in the gym that he always had set up. She leaned against the doorframe, arms folded as she watched him attack a punching bag. He wore a pair of sweatpants, and his body glistened with sweat.

Since their unexpected door visitor something had been bothering him, and she didn't know what. Over the past four days she had seen how distracted he'd been when he didn't think she was looking. What Bain didn't realize, she was always looking at him and always curious about what was going on in his head. Michael was gone. Her past life was behind her, and with Bain she saw a future with the two of them. It was weird considering he was a contract killer, but there were worse things to have in a relationship.

"You look beautiful like that," Bain said, turning with a smile. He headed toward her, leaning down to grab a bottle of water. The moment he was in front of her, he pressed a kiss to her lips, and then pulled back to take a long swig. She couldn't resist admiring his neck as he swallowed, and then she felt like a bit of creep for watching him.

"Morning," she said.

"Morning."

She placed a hand on his chest. His heart was beating normally. He hadn't even exerted himself yet. "I was hoping you'd be in bed this morning." She slid her hand down his chest, resting at the waistband of his pants. He wasn't wearing any boxer briefs.

He covered her hand with his. "I had a few things I had to do." He didn't stop her as she slid her hand inside his pants, and found his cock. The moment she touched him, his dick started to get hard. She loved that. Any doubts she had about them left her mind because of his response to her touch.

"A few things that are more important than this?" She ran her thumb over the tip of his dick, watching as he groaned. The veins in his neck seemed to stand out. "Why do you always come here first?"

"I have to keep up with my training." He moved her so that she was pressed against the wall. His hand was on her waist, moving up to cup her breast. She released a gasp as he pinched her nipple, and then tugged open her shirt. The bottle of water dropped to the floor, forgotten as his lips tugged on her nipple which he'd exposed.

Sinking her fingers into his hair, she watched as

she lapped at the firm bud. He glided his tongue across the valley of her breasts, taking in the second one. He didn't let the first nipple go unattended as he covered it with his hand, kneading her soft flesh.

She pressed her thighs together as arousal rushed between her legs. He kept her in a constant state of arousal. She craved his touch more than she did air.

At thirty-six years old, she had never thought about sex all that much until Bain had claimed her as his own.

"You're doing that thing to distract me."

"Is it working?" he asked.

"You can't keep your secrets forever."

"I can try."

She whimpered as he dropped to his knees and lifted one of her legs, placing it over his shoulder. His fingers caressed up the inside of her leg. She cried out as he filled her pussy with a single finger, his thumb stroking over her clit.

"You want my mouth on this pretty little pussy?" he asked.

"Please, Bain."

"I love it when you beg. There's no other man who will ever give you what I can. Only I can make you feel this good."

"Please." She needed his mouth, and then she needed his cock. She had to have something because she couldn't think straight.

His tongue flicked across her clit, and she cried out. He placed both of his hands at her hips, keeping her standing. Her pussy felt empty, and she wanted him, only him.

"Bain, please…"

"I know, baby. Let me take care of this for you."

She had wanted to take care of him inside their

bed. Staring down at his head, she ran her fingers over his cropped hair, as she began to thrust her pussy against his mouth. He made her so wanton. She would have never tried to seek her own pleasure before. Bain moved his hands from her hips, gripping her ass so tightly that she knew there would be bruises where his fingers were.

"You taste so damn good." He slid his tongue down, filling her pussy, and fucking her with it. When she thought she was close to orgasm he stopped, moving back to her clit, sucking and nibbling on the hard bud.

"Please, Bain," she said, once again.

"What do you want, baby? Tell me and I'll get it for you."

"I want you inside me. I need you."

Within seconds he had moved her toward one of the machines that he used for weight lifting. He sat down and then moved them so that she was straddling him. His cock was already out, hard, and ready. "Take me, Scarlett."

She had wanted to be on top of him again for so long now but always held off for fear of upsetting him, or bringing back memories he'd rather forget. "You're sure."

"I'm completely sure."

Wrapping her fingers around his length, she watched the pre-cum ooze out of the tip. Placing his head at her entrance, she returned her gaze to his, and lowered herself down onto his dick. With every inch that she took inside herself, she watched as his eyes seemed to go a little darker, the pupils dilating, and his cock pulsing within her. His reaction set off a new kind of power that she didn't want to give up.

"You have no idea what you do to me," he said.

He palmed her hips, moving down to her thighs, gripping them tightly. She loved how big and rough his hands were. They only aroused her more with his touch. He went back to her hips and slammed her down taking the rest of him so that he was seated to the hilt inside her.

She cried out. He wasn't a tiny man, and his cock at this angle seemed to go far deeper than before.

"This is where I'm always supposed to be," he said.

Licking her dry lips, she placed her hands on his chest. "You've been lying to me, Bain," she said.

"Don't talk about it now."

"You use sex against me all the time. I figure now is the perfect time to find out what has been bothering you." She moaned as he pinched her nipples and then stroked them with his finger. Closing her eyes, she basked in the sharp bite of pain but didn't get off track.

"We don't need to talk about this."

"I think we do. In fact, I know we have to talk about this. You can't keep hiding it from me." She rolled her hips and watched as his jaw clenched. "Who was at the door?"

"You're not going to win this, Scarlett. Let's just enjoy this."

"Bain, we've not known each other very long, but even in that short time, I know when something is bothering you. You're training hard, harder than I bet you ever have before. We rarely leave the house, and there're guns everywhere. What's going on? You can't hide from me or whatever is bothering you. I don't want you to live in fear."

She rocked against him and struggled not to close her eyes because they were both still aroused. It was crazy, and insane. He held her tightly, and when she would have stopped to question him, he took control and made her fuck him even harder. He pulled her up and down on his cock, making her take him even more.

"I won't let them take you away from me. Touch yourself, Scarlett. Let me see and feel you come apart."

She wanted to deny him, to argue and tell him no, but instead, she reached down and stroked her clit as he continued to pound inside her. She was supposed to be in charge, but against his strength and the pleasure, she couldn't fight it.

Just a few strokes to her clit, and she came apart, yelling his name and whimpering as he slammed up inside her. There was no way she was going to be without bruises as he held her so tight. It was almost as if he was afraid of letting her go.

Within seconds, Bain joined her, flooding her with his cum as his cock pulsed within her. She collapsed on his chest, refusing to move. She didn't care if they made his exercise equipment dirty. She wasn't moving, not an inch.

"I was an idiot. I hurt Boss, and now, because of my mistake, he's coming after you. I'm training to make sure that I can protect you. That's why I won't sleep in, and why I've got weapons around the house. I'm preparing for him. He'll strike when I least expect it. I can't let anything happen to you. I won't."

Wow, she didn't expect that. Her days were possibly numbered, and as she looked at Bain she saw fear in his eyes, which was so strange coming from him.

****

Killian's warning had to be taken seriously. Boss wasn't a man to do things half-assed, and Bain knew without a doubt that he would strike out and hurt him. The only way to hurt him was to do it with Scarlett. He shouldn't have shot him, and he regretted that, now more than ever.

Scarlett hadn't said anything to him since he had told her the truth. She stood in his kitchen, dressed in one of the many dresses he'd bought her, the fabric molding to every single curve and turning him on as she silently cooked them dinner.

After their lovemaking in the morning, she had climbed off and showered. Then he'd followed her around the house as she cleaned everything.

Was she quieter than usual?

Crap, he couldn't stand this, not knowing her thoughts or what to do.

"Talk to me, Scarlett."

She glanced over at him. "What would you like me to say?" she asked. "Everything seems kind of lame and silly." She chuckled. "I'm just doing dinner." She tilted her head to the side, staring down into the pot.

"Just talk to me. You can say anything, but don't give me this silence any longer. I can't stand it."

Once again her gaze was on him. "I'm trying to figure things out. This guy, he's going to hurt me because you shot him? Why didn't he shoot you back?"

"I don't know. Boss doesn't react. He never has. He gets even."

She poured two cans of tomato sauce into the pan and stepped away. With her hand on her hip, she leaned on the counter, staring at him. "What do you want me to do, Bain? You're scared of Boss?"

"No! I'm not afraid of him."

"Then what are you afraid of?"

He stared at her. "You really don't know?"

"Know what?"

"Boss has never frightened me because I've never had anything to lose, don't you get that? He's … he's the owner of Killer of Kings."

"And that makes him worse than any of you?" she asked.

"He's got a body count that no one can even begin

to imagine. Killing is an art form to him, Scarlett. Lisa was just a number to him. He has to get the job done no matter what."

Tears filled her eyes, and he hated that he had brought up her friend.

"I've never had anything to lose, and I can't stand the thought of anything happening to you, baby. I can't."

"You can't live like this, Bain. You're going to kill yourself. You have to rest."

He shook his head. "No. The moment I stop being on my guard, he'll come for you, and I told you, I can't have you leaving my side. I won't … it's not happening."

She turned back to the stove, and he watched as she stirred some seasoning into the pan. "I never for a second thought I could be this happy," she said.

"Scarlett?"

"No, you can let me speak. I've heard enough of what you said. In your own words, you have said that Boss won't kill me."

"No."

"He'll just hurt me."

"I'm not going to let that happen."

"Would it be so bad to let him do that? To let him do whatever he wants?"

Bain gritted his teeth. He got up from his seat and rounded the counter so that he was in front of her. Cupping her face, he forced her to look at him. "I'm not going to let you to be hurt because of me."

Tears shone in her eyes. "Viper, he hurt for you as well, didn't he?" She covered his hands with her own. "I love you, Bain. I know it makes everything else crazy and even myself, but I love you. I want to spend the rest of my life being happy. The last four days, they've been perfect. The best days of my life so far, and saying that at thirty-six years old, is kind of sad. You make me happy.

Do I make you happy?"

"More than anything. You know that." He'd never thought he'd be happy or find a woman he trusted as much as he did Scarlett. It was why he was freaking out over Boss. Normally, he'd just take the guy out, but killing Boss came with consequences, and he wasn't about to create more pain. He had to wait it out. Even as he'd been training, he'd been trying to figure out how to bargain with the devil. What could he possibly want in place of Scarlett? There had to be something.

Killian was a strange kind of guy. He was a hardened killer, but unlike everyone in the business Bain had ever known, Killian had morals. There were jobs he wouldn't take, and even jobs he'd been known to intervene on. More than once Killian had gotten on Boss's bad side.

"Then let me do this for you. If Boss comes, he does." She went on her tiptoes and pressed a kiss to his cheek.

His cell phone rang and interrupted their moment. Glancing down, he saw it was Viper. "I've got to take this."

"Go ahead. I'll finish up dinner."

He didn't go far. Sitting down in a chair in the doorway, he watched Scarlett work as he took the call. She loved to cook, and he'd never eaten so well in his life.

"What have you called to warn me about now?"

"For a guy who has a revenge-seeking Boss on your hands, you'd think you would be nicer."

"Like you said, I've got a revenge-seeking bastard on my hands. I'm not in the habit of making pleasant conversation."

"You know he's going to come," Viper said. "It's only a matter of time."

"He's not getting anywhere near her. I will kill him, Viper. Be sure of that."

"Why don't you stop being a pussy, and call him. Talk to him."

"Why would I do that?" he asked.

"Reason with him. Boss is many things. He's a killer and a businessman. See if there's anything you can offer him that he wants."

Bain closed his eyes, suddenly feeling exceedingly tired. He'd not been sleeping well, and besides the few hours he allowed himself, he was starting to wear thin.

"Is that all you called me about?"

"Bain, other killers are taking bets on how long you last in this business. They think Boss is going to kill you. Don't prove them right, okay? I don't want to lose you."

"Nothing is going to happen to me. I'll be perfectly fine." He hung up the phone, not wanting to hear any more of Viper's miserable voice.

His old buddy had a point though. The only thing he hadn't done was talk to the man himself. What harm would it do?

Scarlett was still dealing with dinner. Scrolling through his contacts, he found the number for Boss and dialed.

It rang several times before Boss finally answered.

"I wondered when you were going to call."

"Yeah, well, I've been waiting for you."

"I see Killian was dealing with his moral compass again. That is going to cost him."

Bain gritted his teeth. "What do you want?"

"I'd say with the fact you're calling now, I bet I've got Viper to thank for this, right?"

This was why Boss would forever be on fucking top. He knew shit that no one else ever did.

"What will it take for you not to come after Scarlett?" he asked.

There was laughter over the line. "Oh, Bain, there are times I question why I wanted you as part of the team. You're always so quick to judge."

"She had no part in any of this. Your beef is with me."

"On that you are correct, but you see, years have taught me that a way to get a message across is to hurt the ones close to the person."

Bain closed his eyes. It had been years, since he was a child, since he had begged for anything. "Please."

"Oh, what is this I hear? You're begging me now, is it?" Boss laughed, this time even louder than before. "I find this so fucking funny. I never thought anything would get the precious Bain to beg."

"I'll do anything. Whatever it takes, just don't harm her. Take me, fuck with me, I don't give a shit."

"Bain, I'm the boss. I say what goes, and when I'm ready, nothing will stop me from taking her. She'll bear my mark, and every time you see it, you'll know that you did it to her."

Boss hung up, and Bain yelled, throwing his cell phone across the room, watching as it smashed into pieces.

He spun around as Scarlett placed a hand on his shoulder. "It's okay," she said.

"No. It's not going to be okay." He gripped the back of her neck, holding her close. Kissing the top of her head, he tried to think of anything that would stop Boss coming after her.

*Fuck! Fuck! Shit! Fuck!*

Scarlett didn't say anything more to him about

that. They shared dinner, washed the dishes together, and then sat down to watch a movie. Neither of them spoke about Boss or his threats. Bain had cleaned away the broken phone and dumped it in the trash.

After watching a movie, he'd taken her upstairs and made love to her. Once again they had the long drawn out battle of who would fall asleep. He won. He always won, and he watched her sleep. Her light snores were sweet music to his ears. Placing a hand on her back, he felt her back rise and fall with each indrawn breath.

"I will protect you for the rest of my life. I can't lose you, Scarlett. You're the only thing that is good in my life. The only thing I want to keep."

He hated that he had fucked up, and there was no way to take it back. After the life he had lived, he'd promised himself he wouldn't feel helpless again, and yet here he was, helpless to save the woman he loved.

Boss would hurt her, and unless Bain could find something to appease the monster in Boss, it would mark her for the rest of her life. He knew about scars. He had more than any man he knew, and he didn't want that for Scarlett.

For the next week, their life remained the same, going through the same motions. He slept for a few hours, trained, ate, spent time with Scarlett, and then they ate again, made love, and he watched her sleep.

Exhaustion was a horrible thing, and on the eighth night, Bain lost his battle with Scarlett. He fell asleep, and even as he drifted, he promised himself it would be but a few moments.

When he woke up, Scarlett was gone, with a note on the bed.

Picking it up, Bain felt sick to his stomach.

"*Revenge is a dish best served cold. Sweet dreams. Boss XXX.*"

## Chapter Eleven

Scarlett had gotten up in the middle of the night to use the bathroom. Instead of the en-suite, she used the one in the hallway. She made sure to be extra quiet because Bain needed sleep in the worst way. When she came out of the bathroom, a huge man dressed in black wrapped an arm around her waist, slapping his hand over her mouth. At first, she kicked and struggled, until she realized what was going on.

This was the day Bain had been dreading.

Scarlett saw it differently. It was her chance to bring peace to her man, an opportunity to ensure they could live their lives with a clean slate. Boss wasn't going to kill her, just hurt her, and she wasn't afraid of pain. She'd been through so much with Michael, that she'd become immune to physical abuse, learning how to go numb.

The man forced her through the house, with his hand still over her mouth, not that she'd scream. If Bain woke up, he'd do anything to protect her, even get himself killed, and she wouldn't risk that. Once outside in the cool night air, he forced her in the backseat of a car and got in beside her, slamming the door shut.

"Watch how you handle her. If Bain finds out you hurt her, he'll fuck you up," said the driver. As the car sped away from the old farm house, she couldn't help but think of Bain asleep in their bed. She loved him so much. Although she was glad she could finally get this nightmare over with, she couldn't help but feel nervous. Boss had been described as a soulless monster, capable of anything. What if he didn't just hurt her, but tortured her? Her nerves fired hot as she imagined some of the gruesome things she'd seen on crime shows.

"No screaming? That's nice for a change. I was just about to get out my syringe to knock you out," said her kidnapper.

They drove in silence. Awkward silence. She had so many questions, but was afraid to speak up. She'd remember Boss anywhere, but he wasn't here. These were delivery boys, deadly ones, but they probably weren't allowed to hurt her.

"You're not Boss," she finally said.

"Were you expecting him?"

"Actually, yes. So you don't have to worry about me putting up a fight."

"Good to know," he said. The man looked at his watch. "You'll get to see Boss in about eighteen minutes."

She sat back and tried to put up a stoic front. There was no way she'd give these assholes the satisfaction of seeing her fear. The driver never spoke again, and the guy beside her scrolled through his cell phone, ignoring her. She took in the shadowed surroundings as they drove, trying to memorize where they were going. She was surprised they hadn't blindfolded and gagged her. It made her wonder if this was a one-way trip.

When they neared the city marina, her heart raced. For some reason she thought they'd be heading to Boss's house, some overpriced mansion in the suburbs. This was so much worse. But she reminded herself Boss wasn't going to drown her because this was about revenge not murder, or so she hoped.

"Bring her inside," said the driver after pulling into the deserted marina, surrounded by skids and containers. They were so isolated, but she had to be brave. This was no different than taking the interview with Semenov on her own. She did what she had to do, putting her own insecurities to the side.

The kidnapper opened her door and pointed away from the car so she'd exit. Scarlett did as she was told. The worst part of this was probably being in her cat pajamas.

They took the metal staircase in one of the buildings to the upper level. It was some type of control room with wall to wall windows looking over the docks and loading areas. Everything was deserted. The lights in the room were off, only the glow from the outside flood lights filtering inside. When she heard a door click closed, she turned around and saw that the kidnapper had left.

"Nice to see you again."

She looked around, not finding the source of that deep voice. Then a light flicked on and she saw Boss sitting in a chair in the far corner. He stood up and casually walked toward her. He wore all black, his shirt partly unbuttoned revealing the edges of his tattoos. Today his long black hair was pulled back in a low ponytail.

"You got what you wanted," she said, making sure her voice didn't tremble.

He shook his head. "I'm not a monster, Scarlett. Despite what you might hear, I'm just a businessman doing a job."

The researcher in her wanted to know his story, how he managed to run such a massive illegal empire. People fascinated her, good and bad. His life must have been just as tragic as Bain's, maybe worse, or was he a complete psychopath?

"Businessmen don't break the law," she said.

He chuckled. "I thought you were smarter than that. Have you ever met an honest businessman? They screw the system, sell their souls for the almighty dollar."

"What about you?" she asked. "How are you different?"

"Never said I was." He winked, walking to the massive control panel.

Scarlett's mind was working on overdrive, trying to think of ways to make him let her go. "Breaking and entering has very stiff penalties," she said, realizing how lame her threat was considering he was the hitman of all hitmen.

He scoffed. "I own the marina, Scarlett. I own more than you can imagine. I have more money, property, and pussy than any man could want."

"Does that make you happy?"

He smiled, leaning against the counter to stare at her. "You're smart. And the reporter in you is strong. It's the reason I told Bain to put a bullet in you. I knew you'd be a problem."

"I love him. I wouldn't do anything to get him into trouble, even if he is a killer."

"Interesting."

He cracked his knuckles, and a shiver ran down her spine.

"You don't have to hurt me," she said. "Bain was just protecting me, and he regrets what he did to you. People make mistakes, you know."

"Ah, the gunshot." He unbuttoned the rest of his shirt and pulled the material over one shoulder. The man was all corded muscle, and there was no hiding the huge, healing scar where Bain had shot him. She cringed. "Another for my collection."

She swallowed hard. "Fine. Shoot me back as payment for Bain's mistake. Will that make you feel like more of a man? I'd think someone in your position would be past pissing contests."

Scarlett waited for him to strike, bracing herself,

and not giving a shit anymore.

Boss pulled his shirt back on, laughing out loud. Genuine laughter. *What the hell is happening?*

"I like you, Scarlett. You've got more balls than some of my men. And I know Bain. He's a hard head, and if I hurt you, he won't stop until he kills me. But I have a reputation to uphold, and weakness is like blood to the sharks."

She was going to offer him something else so he could save face, but she had nothing. Scarlett had no money, no status, and she wouldn't give him her body. "I have nothing to trade or bargain with. I've been through a lot, so whatever you need to dish out, just do it."

"You have been through a lot of shit, haven't you? What was worse, the beatings or the miscarriage?"

"Fuck you."

"Feisty." He smirked. "I wouldn't have pegged you as a good match for Bain. Then again, after what he's been through, I didn't really think he'd hook up with any woman for more than a night."

"You know about him then?"

"Killer of Kings knows absolutely everything, and, darling, I *am* Killer of Kings."

"Then why would you want him to suffer more than he has? The things he's been through are unreal. I get you have this image to maintain, but shit, don't you have a heart?"

Boss stared at her, no emotion in his eyes this time. She expected more laughter, but his personality could apparently do a complete one-eighty in the blink of an eye. "You're brave," he said.

"I'm a researcher … or I was. There are certain things I believe in, and that includes standing up for what's right. And since I met Bain, I also believe in protecting the one I love. You kidnapped me, but I would have come on my own free will."

He clapped his hands, slowly, methodically. She was hypnotized, the whole scene eerily disturbing. "I could use a woman like you."

"What's that supposed to mean?"

"Not whatever the fuck you're thinking," he said. "I'm talking about work. You're good at research, intel, judging character. I'm surprised you hadn't moved up higher at your job. I hear you were slated to be cut."

"I knew it," she said, cursing her old boss. "I was the brains behind half the stories on the news, but I never got credit because of my age, my weight, my looks. It's frustrating."

"I imagine it would be. Fortunately, we don't go by the same standards at Killer of Kings. Shit, you've seen some of my men, most of them are fucked up. If they do their job well, that's all I care about."

Scarlett was oddly intrigued. She'd never been appreciated on the job and knew getting another opportunity as a reporter would be the same drama, the same bullshit image that she didn't fit. Did she dare to take Boss up on an offer? Was he even offering her anything?

She heard a scuffle outside the door, and it got Boss's attention. He pulled a gun from the back of his pants. "Move away from the door," he said.

Scarlett did as told, not wanting to get in the middle of a potential crossfire. The door burst open, and her kidnapper, another big guy, and one of the men from Michael's house piled into the room, all with guns drawn.

"Why are you three idiots in here? Didn't I say I wanted to be alone with our special guest?"

"Boss, your beef is with Bain, not the girl."

"Killian, you're really proving to be a fucking headache," said Boss. "And your loyalty is getting questionable. Why don't you wait in the SUV like I asked you?"

"You know I'll do anything for you, but sometimes I can't keep quiet. Like now."

Boss held out his arms, one hand holding a gun. "I'm being a fucking gentleman. Does she look injured? Is she in distress? No. We're talking like civilized people. Now get the fuck out before you do piss me off."

Two of the men left on command, but Killian stayed. "Bain will be looking for her before long."

"Your point?"

"He'll fucking kill you this time, a bullet right to the heart. Maybe a head shot," said Killian before he left the room.

Scarlett felt like an outsider looking in. She didn't want Bain to do something stupid that could get him killed. Surely Boss could be reasoned with. Then again, he'd killed Lisa in cold blood.

****

"She's fucking gone!" Bain shouted.

"Bain?"

It was just after five in the morning, so he guessed Viper had been asleep. His alarm had gone off and instead of finding Scarlett in bed beside him, he'd found a note. Boss had her, and only God knew what the bastard planned to do.

"Boss has Scarlett. I don't have a clue where he's taken her."

"You knew this would happen," said Viper. "He wants to level the playing field. You never should have shot him."

"I already got that much. I don't need to be fucking reminded."

Bain felt like a caged tiger, pacing his bedroom with a volatile energy building stronger by the second.

Boss had been in his house, gotten through his security system, and taken his woman from right under his nose. He felt like a failure, powerless, and also ready to bring a firestorm of pain to Boss.

"What do you want from me? I'm out of the life, and besides, Boss won't listen to anything I have to say."

"I just need to know where he's taken her," said Bain.

"I've been to his house, but it's hours from you, and I doubt he'd bring her there. Think this through before you do something stupid."

"Who would know where he's taken her?" asked Bain.

"Killian's the one watching his back these days. He'd probably know."

"Okay, talk to you later. I've got shit to handle—"

"I'm not letting you go in this alone. You're too damn impulsive for your own good. Meet me at old church off Tobermory in an hour. I've got your back."

Bain turned off his spare cell and tossed it on the bed. His mind was focused on one task. He'd obsessed over this moment for over a week, and the second he let down his guard, the unimaginable happened. After a lifetime of horrors, he finally had something worth living for—only to lose it just as quickly.

Bain showered, dressed, and began to pack up his arsenal. By the time he left his house he was so strapped with heat, that he was a one-man killing machine. He met Viper at the old church. The sun was now coming up, the sky morphing from navy to light blue. The city in the distance was huge, housing millions of people. Where was Scarlett?

They both exited their vehicles. "Hey, how you doing?" asked Viper.

"Remember when you came to the Henshaw

Corporation to kill Bernard Sutherland? You'd changed. You were ready to do anything for Pepper, for one woman," said Bain. "I thought you'd gone weak, forgotten your training, lost your fucking mind." He chuckled. "Now I understand."

"We'll get her back, Bain. Boss is crazy, but he's not dumb enough to kill your woman. He wants you working for him. You're rough around the edges, but you're damn good at what you do. He knows that."

"If one hair on her head—"

"We'll get her back," Viper repeated. He pulled out his cell and dialed a number. "Killian?" Viper handed Bain the phone.

"Where's Scarlett?" he shouted.

"Right now? Alive. For how long, I don't know."

"Where is she dammit?"

Killian exhaled into the phone. "You know I can't tell you that, but I'll do what I can to try and keep Boss from hurting her. That's all I can do."

"Why do you give a shit?"

"I don't, but she's innocent. If anyone should be flogged, it's you, not her." There was silence on the other line. "Less than ten minutes away? Not smart. You should stay the fuck away if you want your girl to live. If you show up, Boss'll go apeshit, and you know what that means."

"Tracking us, you little fuck? Watch your back." Bain hung up the phone.

"You should go back to your wife, Viper. You wanted out of this life, and I don't want to drag you back in."

"You're the only other person I care about besides Pepper. Like I've said before, I'll always be there for you."

"Shit's about to get ugly. You're probably rusty,

and this is too important for me to babysit."

Viper frowned, shaking his head. "It's like riding a fucking bike. You never forget." Car brakes screeched on the road next to them and the doors opened, disturbing the early morning hush. "Duck," said Viper.

The shot rang out, and the first body of the day hit the ground with a thud. Bain looked up a Viper, but his friend was already aiming at the next guy.

A second car stopped, the hitmen hiding on the opposite side of their vehicle. Bain and Viper took shelter in the archway of the church. "Just like the good ol' days," said Bain.

"I've missed this. Don't tell Pepper."

They had a laugh together, and Bain wasn't sure if he was closer to crying. If Boss had sent these assholes to kill them, maybe Scarlett was already dead.

## Chapter Twelve

"You want me to work for you?" Scarlett asked.

Boss nodded. "I've done a lot of digging on you. You were going to be cut from your job, and that little prick really thought he could do things without you." He was talking about her boss. "Did you know in recent weeks that paper has had a massive decline in sales?"

"It has?"

"Yes. You haven't been around to guide the stories, and now people are going to start realizing the truth, that they lost their best asset."

"But I'm not even a reporter. Why would you want me to work for you?" None of this made any sense.

"Reporters are like parasites. The moment they scent a story, they just can't help themselves. They smell something bad even before a damn dog does, and reporters are rarely swayed. You're not a reporter, you never were. You're a researcher, the real brains behind the stories. What kept you interested in Bain in the beginning was understanding his story, am I right?"

She licked her lips and averted her gaze.

"Don't worry, Scarlett. None of us have secrets here. You were intrigued by Bain, and then you fell in love with him. You learned secrets that I probably don't even know about."

"You said you know everything."

"I'm talking about the personal shit. I know what that boy went through, from a child up to when he was a man. I get it, and I get his pain, Scarlett."

Boss leaned against the console, staying perfectly still. She had never seen anyone so poised before. He emanated confidence and strength.

"You see, the thing about reporters is they're

always there. No matter how much you try to fight them off. They can get past security, and often sweet talk people into getting their way, or just blend into a crowd. I don't want you to go back to your life of reporting. I want you to work for me, but to do what you do best, get the information I need, and get out. You're damn good at finding shit out, and that information is always valuable in my line of work."

Scarlett hated that she savored his praise about her work. She never actually got it at work, but knowing someone saw what she had value was so damn nice.

"If I do this—"

"We'll have our eye for an eye," Boss said, interrupting. "I got shot, so now I want something in return. Recruiting you, having you under my control, that will deal with possible rumors that I'm weakening. I don't need to be dealing with that shit."

"You must have access to the top of information already."

"Sometimes I need ground stuff, and as you can see from my men, they don't exactly blend in well. Half of the women want to fuck them."

Jealousy hit her hard. The thought of another woman touching Bain made her seethe. If she did this, she'd be helping Bain, helping them. She also liked that her work would actually be appreciated, because being a reporter had been her childhood dream. "I won't kill."

"Honey, I have professionals for that."

"So, I do this and no one else gets hurt? No grudge against Bain?"

"Oh, I did want one more thing, but I've already gotten it," Boss said, holding up his cell phone. "I just got a nice little message from Viper."

He pressed a button and a man's garbled voice came over the line. "Damn it, Boss, I told you to leave the fucking woman alone. This is Bain's one chance at survival. If anything happens to her you'll lose him forever. I'll lose him. Look, I'll come back to make this right. Okay? I'll work a few assignments…"

Boss clicked the off button on the cell phone. "All it takes is a little push in the right direction to get what you want."

The echo of gunshots had her jerking back a little. She had been so interested in the conversation, she had forgotten everything else. She'd been pulled into a different world, and it would take a lot before she was used to this chaos.

"They're a little early. It would seem you're well loved, Scarlett. For what it's worth, putting Michael into a grave was a job well done."

"You killed Lisa."

"Killer of Kings is my life. I'll always do what needs to be done." he said. Boss took a deep breath, pushing off from the console. "I'm sorry that you lost your baby. I know that must have been difficult."

Who was this man? One moment he was a monster, the next, offering his condolences on a baby she never got the chance to hold, but she still loved.

"Bain would make a good father," Boss said. "Please, don't take this personally." He grabbed his gun and pointed it at her head.

Their civilized conversation had come to an end.

The door burst open, and there stood her man. He looked damn fierce, but the moment he caught sight of the gun against her head, he stopped dead. She saw fear in his eyes.

Viper and the man with him before at Michael's house were also with him.

"You know, if you'd waited a couple of hours, I was going to deliver her back," said Boss.

"Cut the bullshit, Boss. Just tell me what you want, and I'll give it to you. You want more *clean* hits. I'll do them. Just don't hurt her." She heard the pain in Bain's voice and saw the worry in his eyes. Bain truly did love her, and seeing her like this was hurting him. She would do anything and everything for him.

Boss sighed, and he removed the gun from her head. "Now that we're all here, I think it's easy to say that I got what I wanted. Viper has agreed to come back on board, and I already have several jobs already lined up. Scarlett here, has agreed to help in some information gathering."

"You're not using my woman for your fucking work. She's not a damn killer."

Scarlett went to Bain, placing a hand on his chest as she smiled up at him. "I want to help."

"You're not a killer," he said.

"And I won't kill." She turned toward Boss. "I won't help kill innocent people."

"I'm not stupid, Scarlett. I only want you to handle the more … dangerous people. I'm sure Bain will make sure that you won't get hurt," Boss said.

"You son of a bitch. Just get your fucking payback with me, right now, and leave her out of this." Bain held out his arms, a gun in each hand.

She placed her hand on Bain, stopping him from doing something he'd regret. He was just crazy enough to sacrifice himself for her, and she loved him even more for it.

"It done. It's over. I'm not settling, Bain. I'll be doing what I love. Please, let's go home. We're done here," she said, looking back at Boss. "We're done?"

"We're good for now. And I want an invite to your wedding. Someone needs to give you away."

Scarlett saw that in a dysfunctional kind of way,

he cared.

Bain wrapped his arms around her, and without another word, they left. She glanced back to see Boss watching them. There was something on his face. It was only there for a few seconds, but it looked like envy. Was it envy? No, it couldn't be. Boss was a vicious monster who only cared about power and money. He had recruited her, and now she worked for Killer of Kings.

Even though Bain disapproved, she was actually really excited about her new role. Sitting at home all day while Bain went out and did his thing didn't appeal to her. And she didn't like the idea of women falling all over him, like Boss implied. If she could help, then that was exactly what she wanted to do. She'd get to live her dream, get the credit she craved, and live her life with a man who loved and respected her. What more could she want?

The moment they were near Bain's car, he threw his weapons into the backseat, and grasped her face. "Do you have any idea how fucking scared I was?" he asked. "Nothing can happen to you."

Tears filled her eyes, and she smiled at him. "Nothing did happen to me."

"You made a deal with the damn devil, Scarlett. Do you have any idea what that means?"

"It means that you and I get to fight another day together. It means that you won't lose anything, and you won't have to look at me feeling like you failed. I love you more than anything else in the world, and if I had to sell my soul to the devil, I would do it for you without hesitation." Her tears traced down her cheeks, and she held onto him tightly, never wanting him to go.

"I love you so much, Scarlett. I never knew what love was until I had you." He wrapped his arms around her and kissed her neck. She breathed a sigh of relief having him once again in her arms, alive and well.

"Everything's going to be okay. I promise." She pulled back a little and kissed his lips. "You came for me."

"Of course I fucking came for you. I'd never stop coming for you." Bain held her close as he turned toward Viper. "Thank you. I mean it. Thank you for everything."

Viper shrugged. "Sitting behind a desk all day has lost its appeal. I don't think Pepper will mind too much. She's hinted about me getting in touch with Boss. She clearly knows I'm not cut out for being the standard husband and father."

"She's pregnant?" Bain asked.

"Yeah, she is. We don't know what she's got yet, but fuck, I'm going to be a dad."

Scarlett was happy for them.

Bain stared down at her and smiled. "One day, we're going to have our own good news to share." He kissed the top of her head.

"You want a baby?"

"I want whatever you want. There was a time I didn't think I'd be good for a kid, but with you, I know I'd be the best at everything I set out to do."

\*\*\*\*

*Three months later*

"Don't you dare come in here!" Scarlett screamed at him as he went to open the bathroom door.

"This is my moment, too, woman. I should be in there with you," Bain said, placing a hand on the door. He didn't want to be away from her—Scarlett was his life, his air, his everything. This was a big step for the both of them.

"You're not going to watch me pee on a stick, Bain."

"You think I haven't seen worse?" he asked.

"Ew, I don't need to hear about that stuff right now. I want you to see me as sexy, and this is not sexy. It's gross."

He smiled and leaned against the wall. Tapping his fingers against his leg, he released a sigh. His childhood had been a write-off, and the thought of having a kid of his own, a proper family, was more than he dreamed possible. "Have you peed yet?"

"Shut up, Bain. Aren't you supposed to be killer stealthy and all that? Be patient."

"We've just come back from an assignment, babe. I want to hold you and be with you."

He had been apprehensive about Scarlett working for Boss. Killer of Kings was not known for being the ideal place for a woman, especially not for someone like Scarlett. In the past three months, she had proved him wrong. He was the muscle, the killer, and she had a way of finding information even out of nothing. Bain had lost count of the number of times he had brought her surveillance, and she'd gone through it, finding everything that Boss needed.

The door opened, and there she stood. She looked a little pale. The jeans and shirt she wore, molded to her gorgeous curves, and it made him want to take her right then and there. She took hold of his hand, and they both stared down at the stick.

He twirled the wedding ring around his finger, and he smiled. In a weird kind of way, he was happy to finally be owned by her, to feel her love.

"So how do we know if this is good news or bad?"

"It's not bad news, not at all. We would just have to try again," she said.

Bain loved her enthusiasm and her positivity. She was a breath of fresh air in his life.

"One line we get to try again. Two lines, we did it." She squeezed his hand, and he held her just as tightly. This was their moment, and he hoped more than anything that he had given her what she wanted.

He wanted it, too.

A life with her, a family, a baby. His chest tightened at the thought, and for a split second he panicked that something was wrong with him. What if he couldn't give her what she wanted? What if he was a screw-up because of everything that happened to him?

"Oh my God!" She screamed. "Two lines. We're pregnant, Bain. We're pregnant. We're going to have a baby!"

She threw herself into his arms, and she began to cry. These were not tears of sadness; they were tears of joy. It was as if all the pain she'd held onto from her miscarriage had been healed by this one moment, this new beginning.

They were going to be parents. He was going to be a father.

The monsters in his past would stay there. He was going to be the best damn father and husband in the world.

"I love you, Scarlett."

"I love you, too. This doesn't mean we can't keep practicing though." She winked at him.

Bain shook his head, lifting her up, he carried her toward his bed. "Nope. Not going to happen. This dick is out of commission until the doctor says otherwise. For the next few months, be prepared to be pampered and waited on."

She giggled. "So I get to live like normal then seeing as you do that now?"

He chuckled. "I'm the luckiest man having you."

"No, Bain, I'm lucky, because you're the best

person I know."

The End

**Don't miss:**

*Taking Her Innocence, Killer of Kings, 1*

**www.samcrescent.com**

**www.staceyespino.com**

SAM CRESCENT & STACEY ESPINO

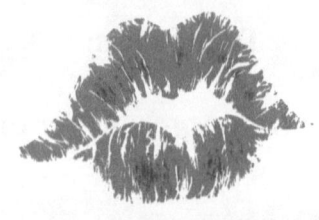

EVERNIGHT PUBLISHING ®

www.evernightpublishing.com